DIARY OF A SHORT-SIGHTEI

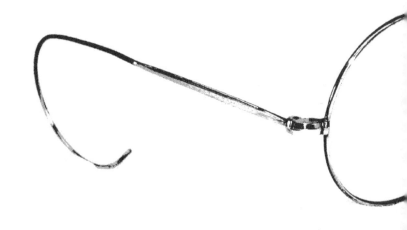

MIRCEA ELIADE

DIARY OF A SHORT-SIGHTED ADOLESCENT

Revised translation by Christopher Moncrieff
with reference to an original translation by
Christopher Bartholomew

First published in 2016 by
Istros Books
London, United Kingdom www.istrosbooks.com

Originally published in Romanian as *Romanul adolescentului miop*

Cover design and typesetting: Davor Pukljak, www.frontspis.lu

ISBN: 978-1-908236-21-0

Printed in England by
CPI Group (UK) Ltd, Croydon, CR0 4YY

Istros Books wishes to acknowledge the financial support
granted by the Romanian Cultural Institute

NATIONAL BOOK CENTRE   ROMANIAN CULTURAL INSTITUTE

With thanks to the Prodan Romanian Cultural Foundation for
supporting the publication of this book.
www.romanianculture.org

PRODAN ROMANIAN
CULTURAL FOUNDATION

CONTENTS

PART I

I

I Must Write a Novel

As I was all alone I decided to begin writing *The Novel of the Short-Sighted Adolescent* this very day. I'm going to work on it every afternoon. I don't need inspiration; I only need to record my life, the life I know; besides, I've been thinking about the novel for quite some time. Dinu knows this: I've been keeping a *Diary* since I was in the Fourth Form[1], when I had freckles like a Jewish boy and studied chemistry in a laboratory in a recess beside the stove. Whenever I felt sad feelings coming on, I would write in my *Diary*. And that *Diary*, which is now two years old, has always had one purpose: to describe the life of an adolescent who suffers from being misunderstood. But this isn't all it contains. My *Diary* flatters me, satisfies my longing for revenge; just revenge on those who misunderstand me.

But the novel will be different. I'll be the hero, naturally. Yet I'm worried that my life – stifled by writing and books – won't be of interest to my readers. For me, everything I've been deprived of, everything I've wished for up in my attic in the restless, sultry twilight, is worth more than all the years my classmates wasted on playing cards, family parties and naïve romance. But what of the reader? Even I realize that the sufferings of a short-sighted adolescent won't touch any hearts if the adolescent doesn't fall in love and suffer. That's why I created a character who I initially called Olga. I told Dinu everything that would happen in the presence of this girl. But he cut me short and begged: 'If we really are friends, please change the heroine's name to Laura.'

At first I was very agitated, because I didn't know exactly *what kind of girl* would touch the heart of a short-sighted adolescent. The only girls I knew were the bootmaker's daughters from next door, and under no circumstances could they be characters in a novel. The oldest, Maria, was skinny and sharp-tongued: she terrorized her brothers, stole green apricots, and screamed at the top of her voice when she chased after trams. The other one, Puica, was fat and grubby. Neither of them would beguile an adolescent; no one knew that better than I did.

Dinu insisted that he could help. He said he had known a great many girls. But how can I write a novel based on a heroine that Dinu knows? I decided that while I was writing, I would think about my cousin. For several weeks I have been questioning her whenever I see her. I told Dinu that I had her under observation.

'If you want to write a novel', she advised me, 'you should make the hero handsome and kind. And call him Silviu.'

But when I told her the title and subject of the novel, she didn't like it.

'There should be two heroes,' she said. 'One handsome, the other ugly. And the title should be: *Love between Children*, or *Spring Flowers*; or *Seventeen*.'

My explanations were to no avail: 'Vally, my dear, this is an intellectual novel, full of internal turmoil', etc. All to no avail. And then I listened to her girlish confidences. It was very useful, because I learnt the vocabulary that girls use, and began to understand something of her dreams, longings, and troubles. It was as if I were listening to confessions that I had heard a long time ago. I remember thinking that my cousin wasn't much different to the heroines in novels, or the sort of character that any lovesick soul could imagine. But how could I be sure that my cousin was really the same person who appeared in these girlish fantasies that she occasionally confided to me?

I know that she yearns to be friends with a kind young girl from a noble family, who would have a large country estate where she lives with her brother, a dark, courageous young man. He would lead them through the forest. He would teach them to hunt, and address them by the familiar form of 'you'. She told me that, one night, she would like to be in the house when it was raided by a gang of thieves. She would grab a revolver and burst into the drawing room just as her friend's brother was being strangled by a gypsy. She would save the brother's life and nurse him back to health in a white bedroom where there was a small table covered with coloured flasks. His parents would be very grateful, and, smiling, would leave them alone together.

At this point my cousin stops. She doesn't want to tell me if she would blush, or shyly withdraw her hand when her friend's brother whispers in her ear: 'I love you!'

I have no idea what else my cousin might imagine about this dark, convalescing boy, watched over by his younger sister and a beautiful friend.

Nonetheless, my novel still has to be written. 'So after this', said Dinu, 'who else will dare let you down?' Perhaps he takes delight in the important role his character will play in the book. He asked me to call the character inspired by him Dinu, and to make him melancholic.

Apart from that I can write whatever I like about him. In fact he insists that I write whatever I like about him. 'But who could possibly find him interesting?' I wondered, just like a real author.

For quite some time, school has been getting steadily worse. My one hope is that my novel will be in bookshops by the autumn. I'll still fail my exams, but it'll be the last time. My teachers will fear me, they will respect me, and in the staff common room they'll protest if Vanciu, the maths master, or Faradopol, who teaches German, decide to fail me.

This week I haven't had much luck; and the end of the final term is getting closer. In French on Monday there was a grammar test. For the past six years, Trollo has only ever tested us on French grammar. And naturally, for six years I haven't learned a thing. This morning I'll get an 'Unsatisfactory' as usual, just like I got in German when Faradopol asked me to summarize the first act of *Nathan der Weise* in German. He has made us speak German since we were in our second year. But he has never actually taught us any German...

This morning I set off for school in a melancholy mood. The chestnut trees were in leaf, the sky was blue, but I hadn't done my homework. I thought: 'I should go to the Cişmigiu Gardens instead.' But I would have been embarrassed by my school bag. And the whole time I would have been terrified that I would be spotted by a master. It saddens me to think that I'm still so feeble, timid, and indecisive. I'd love to have a will of iron, to run away from home, to work in the dockyards, sleep in boats, and explore faraway lands. But instead I'm content to dream and put off victory for later, to fill the pages of my *Diary*. Lost in these gloomy thoughts, I made my way to school. Then Dinu caught up with me and shouted: 'Hey, Doctor!' He calls me this because I'm short-sighted and read books by lamplight. He was ecstatic: he had managed to get a 'Satisfactory' from Vanciu in the oral test.

Today we have to solve... four difficult, intricate questions.

I changed the subject. I told him that my novel would have four hundred pages and be the first in a series called *Dacia Felix*. I know I'll never write this series, but as I had to somehow get my mind off our difficult homework, I told him that the second volume would take place in a hairdressing salon. Dinu laughed.

'That'll be difficult, seeing you've never been a barber. It would be better for the second volume to be set in a girls' boarding school.'

I protested, and reminded him that I didn't know any girls apart from those in our dramatic society, 'The Muse'. My cousin, my only source of inspiration, had been at a girls' boarding school run by nuns for several years; but whenever I ask her about school life she gives me a vexed look.

Nonetheless, at the end of *The Novel of the Short-Sighted Adolescent*, I agreed to include an appeal to all the girls in the Sixth Form, from whom I might obtain diaries, confidences and other intimate details. With material like this, collected 'sur le vif',* I'd be able to produce the second volume.

When we walked into the schoolyard we had to forget all about the future Novel and get a move on, so as to avoid the new assistant master. We ran through the hall and took the stairs four at a time. Once in class I sat in the front row, while Dinu slipped quietly to the back.

I don't have much luck. Other people are lucky with girls, at cards, and at school. I was quite happy to give up girls and cards in order to have luck at school. But I don't.

Just as I finished copying the first and easiest of the four difficult homework questions from my neighbour, Vanciu walked in. When I saw his register with the black cover and white ends, my courage deserted me. He greeted the class in his usual dignified, magnanimous way, confident of his evident superiority and our imminent misfortune. Every time I see him come in I vow I will study mathematics with a passion, if only to be able to confront him with the same serene, assured expression. Sometimes, – when he asks me a question – I secretly make fun of the belly that he tries to hide beneath the folds of his waistcoat. I realized long ago, however, that Vanciu is a Don Juan. If I were a woman and he my mathematics teacher, I'm sure I wouldn't be able to resist him. He overpowers me with his voice, his calm demeanour, his eyes, with the way he solves the questions that he sets us. Yet it irritates me that he's never hit me, because then I could hate him. Instead he just calls me a 'blockhead' whenever I muddle up algebraic symbols, and 'bird brain' when I get nervous at the blackboard, mesmerized by a geometric diagram whose meaning, value, and solution I have to work out.

I prayed, and realized that I didn't know to whom I was praying. I prayed that Vanciu would turn the page of the register and read out the names of boys from the other end of the alphabet; or that he would be summoned to see the Minister of Education; or that the school secretary would bring him an unexpected message, and that we would have the whole period free. Or perhaps I was praying for something else altogether.

But of course he called me to the blackboard first, even though I wasn't the only one in the class who hadn't taken an oral test on this chapter. I walked up solemnly, carrying my exercise book, chalk, and eraser. I didn't want the others to know that I was scared of Vanciu.

Yet the closer I got to the board, the calmer I became. My panic evaporated. I looked calmly into the master's eyes, and when he glanced down at my exercise book I gave my classmates an indulgent smile.

'How many homework questions did we have?'

'Four.'

'Where are they?'

'I wasn't able to finish them,' I replied, humiliated, weighing up the look of disappointment in Vanciu's eyes.

'Do the first one then. Do you know what it is?...'

I didn't know, but I nodded that I did. Vanciu turned his chair to face me, crossed his arms and waited. He understood, and began to dictate the question to me: 'In a circle with radius R, the area created by an arc, where the circle runs around the diameter that passes through an extremity of the arc, has at its base a circle whose surface area is equal to a quarter of the area. Calculate the height x of that area.'

I didn't know where to start. I didn't understand a thing, and couldn't concentrate on the question. I fixed my gaze on some symbols at the corner of the blackboard, and racked my whole body so Vanciu would think I was racking my brains. As I was standing there I said to myself: 'To hell with it!' and then my teeth began chattering. It was all I could do.

Vanciu had decided long ago that I was an idiot, so he was lenient. Although perhaps he had worked out that I was faking, that I never paid attention, and from then on refused to indulge my ignorance. Even so, my stuttering, my absent expression and the way I stared blankly at the blackboard had an effect. Vanciu always helped me.

'Not getting anywhere? We have a circle...'

I remembered that I had drawn a similar one in my exercise book, by tracing round the lid of an inkpot with a pencil. I began to draw a circle, constantly erasing, in order to buy some time. But it was pointless because I didn't understand the question.

'Why don't you do some work, boy?'

'I do, sir. But I get confused...'

'He who works hard...'

'I do work hard, sir...'

'Don't interrupt me!... He who works hard doesn't get confused.'

'I know, sir...'

'Out with it then.'

'I know the answer, but when I...'

'Repeat the question!'

A long pause. The other boys held their breath.

'Go and sit down!'

Relieved, I went back to my desk. In his blue book, for the 15th of May Vanciu inscribed a magisterial and painfully legible 'Below standard'. Attentively and with curiosity I pretended to follow the calculations of my neighbour, a short-sighted Italian with red hair who stubbornly refused to wear his glasses. This boy always did his homework. When questioned he would ramble on and on, with an exasperated Vanciu interrupting occasionally: 'Get on with it then!'

After Vanciu had gone, the other boys surrounded me excitedly and asked: 'What are you going to do now, old chap?'

I told them that I didn't give a damn, because *I knew who I was*, and that they were just common-or-garden Fifth Formers. Whenever I feel humiliated I assert my superiority, and make a point of showing my contempt for others. I know this is childish, but I can't help it. As soon as I've calmed down I always reproach myself.

I walked home with Dinu, and on the way we planned out the chapters for my novel. I didn't want to think about the latest 'Below standard' that I would have to show my mother in the morning. We both came to the conclusion that my only hope was *The Novel of the Short-Sighted Adolescent*, and that I ought to start work on it immediately.

Now, however, after having written all these pages in my notebook, I don't have the courage to begin the first chapter. It's getting late, tomorrow I have some difficult homework to do; and besides, I left my copy of *Bouvard et Pécuchet* on the desk, half-read.

Robert's Glory

Robert once told me that he was very much like D'Annunzio. He has read *L'enfant de Volupté* and *Le Feu*, but always refers to *Il Piacere* as *Il Fuoco*. He comes to see me in my attic, and speaks in melancholy tones of our foolishness and his glory. As I listen, I think of the character that I will base on him. Every now and then I smile: I picture a more complete Robert, altered, transfigured.

Then he becomes suspicious: 'What is it, Doctor?'

I have to quickly come up with a clever response. For some time Robert has suspected that I'm concealing my real opinion of him. He both admires and despises me at the same time. He's always complaining about his weaknesses, which prevent him from attaining real glory.

'If glory were mine, women and money would come to me effortlessly...'

Whenever he talks about women, his face suddenly lights up. In my petulance, which is my usual way of dealing with him, I've caught him out more than once by accusing him of only knowing about women from books and films. He's probably still a virgin. He's an adolescent with no eyebrows, the lips of a peasant girl, a shiny chin, soft cheeks and a broad forehead. I tell everyone that Robert is a beautiful boy.

But I still haven't written anything in the notebooks devoted to my novel. No one is forcing me to produce a detailed portrait of my friend. Even so, I now want to concentrate on Robert, because he'll be an important character in the book, and I need to think about the conflict he'll create.

A conflict between whom? That's what's preventing me from starting the first chapter. I don't have a plot. All I know is that I'm the hero. Of course, the novel will revolve around a crisis at the end of my adolescence. I'll portray and analyse myself in relation to my friends and classmates. But I still have to come up with a *plot*. And since there can't be a plot until there's a heroine, I'll have to include my cousin. But I've tried that, and couldn't manage a single page. I thought I should write in the way other novels are written: florid, exaggerated, with painstaking detail. Yet I soon realized that I was straying from what I was capable of saying, and repeating scenes I had read elsewhere. So once again I put off starting the chapter.

But what will be the subject of my novel? My great love for the heroine, who's on holiday in the country? No. I've never been in love; none of my friends have ever been in love in the way that people fall in love in novels. I'm not sure anyone would be interested in reading about an emotion that the author has never experienced. Besides, I don't think that love is the most interesting thing that can happen to an adolescent. All I know about is our adolescence. But do I *have* to write about that, and that alone? I've experienced far more interesting crises. As have some of my friends. I'll have to find a crisis that links all the heroes and heroines of the novel. If I could find such a crisis, I'd be delighted. It would make my job so much easier.

Because then I could simply introduce the characters one by one; none of them older than seventeen. Without any effort, the central crisis would become crystal clear. And the novel would continue and end as it needed to. When...

But all this is just rambling. I haven't thought of anything natural, or based on real life, that could transform my novel into one with a genuine plot. My friends say that I should write a novel based on the life of schoolboys... A little-known world, undervalued and misunderstood in literature. But I can't describe it accurately. Without wanting to I always change things, exaggerate. Yet the most important thing is that the novel must be published, so I can move up a year at school. It should be a reflection of my soul, without being psychoanalytical; because I don't want it distorted by analysis. And I'm certainly not going to write it in the form of a *Diary*; if I did, I would constantly forget that I was writing for unknown readers. I would concern myself too much with minutiae, and it simply wouldn't work. I wouldn't have the one thing that I'm seeking.

Once I'd finished the last sentence, I stopped. Is this really the only thing that I'm looking for? I don't know, I don't know. There are so many things I could write about, but I don't have it in me to put them down on paper. Whatever the case, I'll tell the truth about myself and other people in my *Diary*, but not in a novel to be read by strangers, who have no need to know about all my shortcomings...

I don't always think like this. But I enjoy contradicting myself. That's why I don't like to go back over old memories.

But I've lost the thread again. The fact is that *The Novel of the Short-Sighted Adolescent* will be a series of vignettes, impressions, portraits, conclusions about school life and the adolescent soul. This might seem dull and analytical; particularly the word 'conclusions'. Yet what is certain is that there will be no conclusions in the novel – because up till now I've never found a use for them. And who will narrate this series of scenes? Should I give up on my hero's romance?

Robert is the starting point, of that I'm certain. What if, in the novel, I make him fall in love with a girl who Dinu also loves... but that's silly. I've never seen either of them in love. Their little dalliances tell me nothing, because they're never changed by them. But once again I've wandered off into a critical debate. My novel will be written without discussions and explanations of any kind.

These sketches for chapter one have come to nothing. I'll try and do some more preparatory work for the novel, and organize my material – about myself and other people – in this *Diary*. Although if my imagination runs riot and starts changing reality, I'll make sure I encourage it, give it some help, and not curb it like I've done in the past. I'll decide whether or not to add extra pages, and provide clarification: 'This passage is untrue; things happened differently.' Come what may, preparations for the novel, draft plans for certain chapters – which will be narrated in the third person – will have to be done systematically. Robert, who I've strayed away from here, is a good pretext.

During Passion Week², I set out with my friend Jean Victor Robert on my first romantic escapade. My friends think I'm shy with girls. The fact is, I suffer because I'm short-sighted and ugly. I'd suffer even more if I were rejected. Because I want to conquer every heart. That's why I'm withdrawn and self-conscious. I dream of the day when, as a result of my work, all eyes will be on me. Until that time, no one will understand how much I suffer.

But all this has nothing to do with romantic escapades. I must make sure not to let such things find their way into my novel.

Bundled along by Robert and Perri, and joined by Dinu, we met up with four girls in Carol Park that afternoon. Everyone knows that Carol Park is where pupils from the lycée go to meet. That was why I was against the idea from the start. I get embarrassed when strangers look at me. There were too many people there, especially couples. But we – us in our school caps and the girls in uniform – were just as suspect as the rest. Nonetheless, that's where we decided to meet.

Robert knew the girls already. He insisted that it was them who had made the first move, and so he had resigned himself to speaking to them. Perri whispered in our ears that they had actually 'picked them up' on the boulevard one evening. Robert had been embarrassed, and talked about French literature. And the girls were enchanted.

Smiling and blushing, we met the girls on a secluded path near the Roman Arena. They introduced themselves, giving their names rather hesitantly. Despite their efforts to appear innocent and make us think that this was their first such rendezvous, they gave the impression of being dressmakers' apprentices. They were wearing simple clothes, and had powdered cheeks, carefully arranged hair and a smattering of lipstick. I heard some wonderful opening gambits, along with silly ironies and encouraging laughter and affectations. But the girls seemed flattered with our company. We strolled along together, two girls and two boys. I was only listening to Robert, who was trying to start a conversation about love and women. The blatancy of Perri's flirting was impressive. Dinu didn't say very much to them, and stared into their eyes, smoking, waiting for his charm to take effect. With a coarse lock of red hair hanging over my forehead, I kept quiet.

It would be pointless to repeat the conversation. After half an hour the ice was broken. We wandered off in pairs, me with the sister of the girl that Robert liked: a brunette wearing a white hat, and with white cheeks and dark eyes. Every time I looked at her I was seized with the unsettling thought that I had already seen her in every group of girls who I had met at every lycée and school event. She was the shortest of the group, and possibly the best behaved. I wanted to prove to myself that I didn't lack courage. I told myself: 'If I haven't put my arm round her by the time I count to ten, then I'm a coward'. The girl kept on blushing more and more furiously. I was pale, gloomy. Talking, talking, talking. All the erotic anecdotes and double-entendres that I could think of were pouring from my lips. The girl, who didn't always catch the hidden meanings, was totally lost. I strode along beside her, gripping her arm, thrilled by her trembling body, by the scent of her hair, her lips.

I said to myself: *'You've got to kiss her!'* I counted to ten. I wasn't brave enough. I scowled, blushed, I was confused and humiliated. The girl dared to say something. And then I forced myself to do it. She shuddered beneath my cold lips that were pressed against her cheek, her hair, her shoulder in its faded cloth.

But I had wanted it too much, and moved too fast. It was still daylight. The other couples could be seen and heard walking about. I made my companion sit next to me beside a spindly fir tree. After almost having to be dragged there, she sat down. She didn't utter a word. She pushed me away with her eyes and hands. I was thinking about who-knows-what act of madness. The girl was terrified. When I kissed her on the lips she leapt up off the seat as if fired from a bow, quickly straightened her dress and rushed away, saying through her tears that she was going to find her sister. All of a sudden my foolish desire to prove that I was an uncouth, uneducated lout evaporated. I went over to her and reproached her for allowing me to kiss her. I don't know what made me lie. I lied to her when I said that I had simply wanted to find out if she was 'virtuous', or if she was like her sister. I began to accuse her sister of all manner of things that made her blush, but it made me feel better. I spoke harshly, hatefully, cruelly about her sister – who I had only just met – insisting that I knew a great many compromising things about her. The girl was on the verge of tears. But I persisted. I told her that she needed to become 'a virtuous girl' again. I took pleasure in torturing her in this foolish way.

We all met up again at the far end of the Arena. The girls kissed and embraced my friends. Jean Victor was delighted. Dinu had perhaps already promised himself that he must do this again. All eyes were on us. I was deathly pale, while she was red-faced from crying. But who knows, maybe the others were jealous of us...

I was furious with myself. I couldn't understand why I had said things that were so out of character, or why I had tormented her in such a ludicrous way, in the name of an overblown moral code that was repugnant as well as alien to my nature. I was completely baffled. It was like something from a nightmare.

On the way back, when I told Robert about my escapade he didn't know what to believe. But after giving it some thought, he said that it was 'interesting', although not very. According to him I should have been much rougher with her, and gone even further. It's odd how he failed to see that I was upset about what had happened.

Ever since that day, I never go with him to meet girls. He started a rumour that I was scared. Perhaps it wasn't far from the truth.

Up till now I've said rather too little about this friend, who is supposed to be an important character in my novel. It's possible that I don't really know him. Robert reads whatever I tell him to, and talks constantly about the books he's read. But – perhaps because of some hidden jealousy – his shallow rhetoric exasperates me. Robert exasperates me, because he's sentimental, dull-witted and conceited. But since this notebook also acts as my *Diary*, shouldn't I perhaps ask myself: am I not just as conceited? I shouldn't be afraid of the answer. I realize that I consider myself superior to everyone. But I keep this hidden within me, and the novel won't reveal it. Robert told me that his quest for glory is the only thing he lives for. I pretended not to understand. And then he began to tell me about D'Annunzio. I envy this Italian, the author of beautiful books, and whose memoires are full of beautiful women. But I'm in no hurry. Before I start craving such extraordinary things, I realize that I will have to work hard and suffer. That's why I despise my friend: because he expects to achieve glory without working for it. Robert is no genius, of that I'm certain. He's simply a beautiful boy, just like a girl, who loves going to the theatre and has plans to write three-act plays. One of his main characters will be based on me. He imagines me in my attic, in a coarse Russian shirt like the one I wear in the summer, with glasses and a disconsolate smile. I'll be a sort of *'raisonneur'*. I'd love to know what Robert thinks of me; not just what he says to my face, but what he actually thinks. I know he's very dismissive of me because he's always saying that I know nothing of life, that I live among books. But he's the one who wastes his time reading novels, and says that he 'has a life'. He's complex, because he has known more girls than I have, and because on Sundays he goes for a stroll along the boulevards. And I'm simple, because I regard these childish occupations as obstacles on the hard and bitter road that I have to travel.

When we get together with our many friends, Robert tells us about his dreams of glory. Sceptically, I ask him if he is doing any actual work to achieve this. He tells us that he reads Balzac, Ibsen, and Victor Eftimiu. We tease him unmercifully, because we both like and dislike Robert.

This is the difference between him and me: one dreams of happiness and waits for it, while the other torments himself to achieve it, without giving it too much thought. And that's another foolish phrase I've just written, but I mustn't cross it out: later on it will remind me how easy it is to draw clear distinctions at the age of seventeen.

In my novel, Robert will have to act and speak in order to make himself known to the reader. He lacks depth and is self-satisfied. I couldn't resist the temptation to tell him about the major part he would play in the book about our adolescence. He listened with feverish anticipation. I said I was going to exaggerate his faults, make him look ridiculous, that I would gather together all the naïve and foolish nonsense with which he had regaled me and our friends over the past year, and put them in the novel. We sat up until well after midnight. Robert complained that I wasn't really his friend, that I would expose myself as a liar if I only wrote bad things about him in the novel.

'And what will you call me?'

'Jean Victor Robert.'

He protested, crying out that I would compromise his career and his glory. That if I had uncovered so many secrets and ugly things about him, our friendship demanded that they should remain between us.

'But I'm writing a novel about morals, a psychological novel,' I lied. 'It has to include real events and real characters.'

'Then why don't you include me in the good parts?'

'Because the author needs a character who looks ridiculous.'

'And why does that have to be me?'

'Because in the novel, Robert is an example of what it is to be ridiculous.'

We parted on bad terms. After thinking it over, however, Robert managed to convince himself that I would never really write a novel where he was portrayed as ridiculous. Ever since then, whenever he talks to me he tries to appear a different person, superior to others and changed by what he has read. He paces up and down my attic with a downcast expression on his face, in exactly the way that I once told him that an anxious, troubled adolescent should walk. He talks to me about *Brand*, a novel he borrowed from me, and tried as hard as he could to be like a Nordic hero.

It would be interesting to make a note of all the masks that Robert has worn for my benefit over the past few weeks, in order to make me change my opinion of him, and prevent me from portraying him as ridiculous.

I pretend to be convinced by these changes. The other boys were amazed; they thought it was just a practical joke. But Robert was so pleased with these new 'characters' that he had adopted that he actually began to believe them. This will require further thought. Because of an allusion I made, Robert has started to believe that he is *another person*. I'm afraid that things might go too far. But when he's all alone in Târgoviste during the holidays, I think he'll go back to being to his former self. He'll forget about Brand and Andrea Sperelli, and again become a dull-witted, beautiful adolescent who yearns for glory.

But here I am, ending these pages of my *Diary* with something of a cliffhanger. When it comes to writing the novel, I'll have to plan my chapter endings properly.

III

A Class Diary

I have always liked to keep a proper, regular *Diary*. I started this notebook on the day I decided to begin *The Novel of the Short-Sighted Adolescent*. But I've got into the habit of writing in it rather too often. Impressions, brief notes jotted down hastily in class continue to fill this private *Diary*. And now this notebook is almost finished. In it I plan to transcribe some of my more detailed observations, especially those that will serve as material for the novel.

I like to re-read my notes whenever I have time, because they are alive and precious to me. Of course, I'll change and exaggerate them in the novel – because if I don't, no one will ever read them.

*

One day at the end of May. In history class, Noisil asked Caleia a question that we had been given for homework. As usual, Caleia didn't know a thing. He stuttered and stammered while trying to hear what Tolihroniade was whispering from behind. (Tolihroniade always whispers the answers so Caleia will do the same for him). The question was about Marco Polo's voyage of discovery.

'What route did he take?'

Caleia thought for a moment. To buy time, he repeated the question: 'What route did he take?'

'Yes.'

'They went around the Cape of Good Hope.'

'At that time it was called something else.'

'So you want me to tell you what it was called in those days?'

'Yes.'

Silence. Tolihroniade's whispers got louder and louder. Finally Caleia heard him.

'It was known as the Cape of Storms.'

'And then where did they go?'

'To Brazil.'

Sniggers.

Caleia looked at his neighbours with hatred and contempt.

'And where did they end up?'

'In Brazil.'

'And what did they discover there?'

'Indian territory.'

'Anything else?'

'What else did you expect them to find?'

*

Pake is going to have to repeat a year. In the Second Form he came top and won a prize, while in the Fourth Form he got a commendation in maths. And now he's going to have to repeat a year. But he's still just as imperturbable, eats as much as always and mumbles to himself the same as before. When asked what happened, he replies: 'I couldn't give a fig!' But if anyone dares to tease him, he swings round with a laugh and punches them.

'It's just my way of having a joke', he says. *'Chacun à sa manière.'*[*3]

He might not have had to repeat a year if Vanciu hadn't caught him in a bar during break, with some sandwiches and a litre of *ţuica*[4] on the table in front of him. He was summoned to the common room. He said the sandwiches were his, but that the *ţuica* belonged to a man who had left without finishing it. He even tried to give a description of the man. Vanciu let him have his say, and when he had finished he reminded him that he had actually paid for the *ţuica*. He was suspended for a week and his mark for behaviour was lowered from 'Satisfactory' to 'Unsatisfactory', a fact that only seemed to worry his parents and the rest of us. Pake still smokes during break and slips a small bottle of cognac out of his schoolbag, taking the odd swig while swearing and good-humouredly punching his friends.

Even though he has to repeat a year, Pake hasn't given up his trips to the Fagaraş Mountains, or camping in the Sibiu forest. If we can't find anyone to come with us to Fagaraş, then the two of us will go on our own, like we did when we first became friends.

*

Music class. Perhaps the last music class of the year. The Director of Music came in carrying a bundle of scores, his new romantic ballad, called 'The Crane', hoping to sell them to us. He spoke in a quiet, mournful voice.

'I have little choice, gentlemen. I had to pay the printers 1500 lei and just want to recover my costs. There's no question of me making a profit... only six lei each.'

He smiled. We each gave him six lei, and laughed at the composer. Then we asked him to play it. The Director sat at the organ and played mournfully, swaying back and forth on the stool. It was an unexceptional melody, one that I had heard before, although I'm not sure where. After he had played it several times, the organ stopped squeaking and he got up from his stool. There was wild applause and laughter. The Director of Music smiled. Then he asked the baritones to come up and practice the choral piece for the end-of-year festival. But he added, in the same quiet voice: 'Gentlemen, if you don't keep the noise down I'll call the Headmaster!' But nobody believed him. Only three baritones stood up.

'Where are the baritones? Didn't you hear me, gentlemen? Will the baritones please come to the front. We only have a few days left before the festival.'

'Oh, give it a rest,' came a voice from the back.

'Who is being so impertinent?'

'Doesn't it stick out a mile!'

'Will you be quiet!'

'Once a thief...'

'...always a thief...'

'...so sayeth the Lord, amen!'

'I shall throw you out of the class!'

'Go on then, I dare you!'

'Stop this instant, you impudent boys!'

'Tu l'as voulu Dandin!'*

'I'm calling the Headmaster.'

'One moron begets another!'

'I shall give all those in the back row bottom marks for bad behaviour.'

'Why are you annoyed, Mr Boloveanu?'

'Why are you so strict with us, Mr Boloveanu?'

'A schoolmaster should be like a father to us.'

'...But his voice is divine.'

'Damn it all!'

Six baritones came forward, leaning on each other and pretending to pick up their scores from the floor. One of them asked if he could be 'excused'. When he was refused permission, he claimed that he wasn't able to sing, and said there was 'real barbarity and abuse of power that went on in this school'. Boloveanu carried on playing the organ, checking the number of baritones out of the corner of his eye.

'Fossil' tried to slip out of the room. He wasn't popular because he had a limp, sneaked on the other boys, was miserly, worked hard, copied his neighbours during tests, was good at chemistry, and – above all – was a Jew. The others called to him from their desks, loud enough for the Director of Music to hear.

'Where do you think you're going, Pǎrtinişeanu?'

'Where are you running off to, Fosilo? Don't you know that the master doesn't allow anyone to leave?'

'Stay in your seat, Fosilo!'

'Why don't you do what the master says?'

Blushing bright red, Pǎrtinişeanu crept back to his desk, where someone was waiting. Caleia, who sat behind him and was reading *Le Petit Parisien*, hit him on the back of the head. The sound of the blow echoed. The baritones, who were still singing, turned to look.

Naturally, 'Fossil' went and told the master after the lesson. Caleia got an hour's detention.

*

Aguletti cried during chemistry today, and invoked the memory of his late father so Toivinovici wouldn't give him an 'Unsatisfactory.' The whole scene made me blush with embarrassment, and clench my fists in exasperation. I was overcome by indescribable feelings of both pity and revulsion for Aguletti, contempt for him and sympathy for the master.

Fănică wished he was as good at faking as Aguletti. Aguletti is a malingerer and a liar. I would gladly lie as well, if I could; but why did he bring his dead father into it?

I think the whole class had the same feeling of excruciating embarrassment.

*

I'd very much like to get to know Dinu, to know him really well, for the purposes of my novel. It's not enough to simply be aware that he's handsome, decent, and intelligent. I can sense that there's something in his soul that eludes the rest of us. Why is it that he is showing less and less interest in chemistry these days? We used to study together at his house, in a makeshift laboratory set up on benches in a small room in the basement. But this year he's virtually forgotten even the most basic formulae. He's not 'passionate' about it anymore, to use one of my favourite expressions. He doesn't do any work. He hardly reads any literature, just goes for walks and sleeps a lot. Dinu has never been terribly industrious, or organized. But now he's completely changed. It might just be a personal crisis. Yet sometimes, when I'm alone, I wonder if this is actually the *real* Dinu, if his passion for science over the last year and a half was nothing but an illusion? What if he were deceiving himself as well as the rest of us all that time, and is only now beginning to realize who he is?

I'm not yet sure what role he'll play in the novel.

*

Robert's eyes hurt from reading too much, and because of the formalin that the classrooms were sprayed with on Sunday. He kept rubbing his eyes, and now they are red and watering. He sat there looking morose, holding a handkerchief to his eyes. I'm sure he sees himself as a character from Ibsen, afflicted by spiritual and physical torments. He wandered around so we would see how much he was suffering, and feel sorry for him. If a master asked him why he was holding a handkerchief to his eyes, he was delighted, and replied in a way that implied that any intelligent person would realize that his eyes hurt because he had been reading too much.

Yesterday he said to me: 'You can't imagine how much my eyes hurt. Last night I read until two o'clock.'

I pretended to be amazed that he read so little, and told him that I never go to bed before three – which was a lie.

*

Maths test. As usual it was a very easy question. But since I didn't know a thing, – because I hadn't learnt anything during the entire year – I stared at it uncomprehendingly. My lack of knowledge began to make me feel miserable. If I had done even a little reading I could have worked it out. Around me the other boys were hard at it. Only Malureanu and Colonas were looking at their exercise books with the same fixed gaze as me. The three of us were the most useless at maths in the class.

Sitting there unable to do anything began to annoy me. I managed to write out a series of calculations that had nothing to do with the subject. It was a question on trigonometry, but all I knew about trigonometry was how to work out if something is a right-angled triangle. I wrote down everything I knew: if I left the page blank I would have got an 'Unsatisfactory'.

During the first term, in order to infuriate Vanciu and get my own back on him for smiling at what he always presumed was my ignorance when I was up at the blackboard, I would close my exercise book and start writing on a sheet of paper I took from my bag. I wrote so Vanciu would see me, and so he would get annoyed because he didn't know what I was writing or why I was writing, and would wonder how I had the courage to do it.

Vanciu watched me, and couldn't believe his eyes. Meanwhile I was delighted to have the chance to analyse myself and take notes about my current spiritual state.

When I'd finished I stuffed the piece of paper into my pocket – where there was already quite a bundle.

If I get another 'Unsatisfactory' at the end of this term, there's no hope for me.

*

A note from 2nd June, when I saw that the boys at the desks in front of me looked sad, weren't talking, and were lost in thought.

See what is happening to our hearts and souls now we have come to the end of the academic year: we are overwhelmed with melancholy. We're exhausted, sick of school, weary of the heat, and yet we're sad because it's the end of the year. We give the impression of being grateful, we laugh and talk, but deep down inside we feel the stirrings of nostalgia. This is perfectly understandable. Perhaps we're thinking about the joys of summer, but it makes us sad when we remember that we'll be *alone*. The prospect of separation dispels the pleasure.

Are we really so attached to each other after six years of being in the same class? Or is there maybe another reason? Perhaps we're downhearted because, after Easter, our holidays never quite live up to what we expected. We imagine that the first few days of the holidays will be a kind of paradise. But they never are. It's simply that, little by little during the last week or so of term we grow accustomed to the joys of freedom, and when the final bell rings we search in vain for this vast, never-ending pleasure. Or at least I've never found it myself. It's true that many of us might appear cheerful and boisterous, but as far as I'm concerned that doesn't mean anything. I've put on the same act many a time...

*

Today, Fănică got a 'Good' in Chemistry. He went back to his desk exhausted, looking shattered; when he apologized for not having brought his exercise book, his voice trembled. After Toivinovici had left, he went up and kissed the blackboard then gave the rest of us a hundred lei for croissants and chocolate. Which was the height of madness, given Fănică's usual miserliness. With the 'Good' that he got in the oral test, he was guaranteed to be average in the class.

Fănică is terrified of chemistry. I'm sure he revises each question at least ten or fifteen times, and then forgets it all the moment he's called up to the board. He's a bag of nerves, as if he's standing in front of the School Inspector. He goes bright red, he stutters, his fingers crush the chalk against the board rubber. He hates Toivinovici and shakes with fright every time the door opens during a chemistry lesson. Surprise written tests bring him out in a sweat, he wriggles around at his desk, gets caught immediately whenever he tries to ask his neighbour even the most trifling question, becomes flustered, spills ink, and writes out the same question at least three times. Several days before a written exam he loses his appetite. The night before he revises until after midnight and wakes up in a cold sweat. He arrives at school weak, confused and exhausted. When Toivinovici walks into the room, Fănică is rooted to the spot and can't take his eyes off him. He only snaps out of it when the register is being taken. And then he gets nervous, impatient, and starts fidgeting, tormenting himself until Toivinovici reads out the questions or gives out the subject of the exam.

If the bell rings before he's finished his work, Fănică goes bezerk. He tries frantically to write down any conclusion that he can think of. During the whole test he writes 'reference material' generally related to the subject in order to fill as many pages as possible, and convince Tovinovici that he has done some work. His conclusions are usually the best part, because they aren't 'reference material.'

Fănică always keeps a packet of headache pills in his shirt pocket. The other boys are fond of him because he's intelligent and timid. He laughs and jokes in every class except chemistry and maths. And he's adept at knowing the best way to apologize to the masters. Yet no one is quite sure why he's known as 'Rooster.'

IV

Among Don Juans

This evening Robert and Dinu came over to my house, and decided we should go for a walk in the Cişmigiu Gardens. Robert was wearing white trousers and shoes with bows; Dinu's jacket was unbuttoned: he had an antelope-skin belt and a silver cigarette case. Neither were wearing a cap or hat. Jean Victor Robert – who considers himself a genius – rested his forehead in his right hand whenever he needed to sit down. Dinu – who girls say is 'good-looking and ironic' – endeavours to be seen as a cynic, a paradoxical Don Juan.

I buttoned my tunic and we went out into the street. Robert sighed, Dinu offered me a cigarette. Robert sighs because he's a genius. He told me one night that geniuses are unhappy.

'Why?'

From the heights of his greater knowledge, Robert gave me a kindly pat on the shoulder.

'You simply wouldn't understand...'

To Robert, I'm just 'the doctor.' I have all the symptoms: I'm ugly, already deformed by short-sightedness and have erudite preoccupations. But Robert the genius was quick to console me: 'We all have our burden in life, doctor...'

Dinu is mistrustful and judgemental. He's suspicious of Robert because he's as handsome as he is, and – although he tells anyone who'll listen that he's not afraid of Robert – this rivalry unsettles him. It became even more conspicuous at a wedding, when Robert's partner, a blonde girl from Târgovişte who had just passed her baccalaureate, gave Dinu a rose from her corsage at the end of the evening. He still keeps it in a casket, along with letters and small coloured bottles. Whenever anyone mentions this, Robert smiles broadly.

It's so childish...

Out on the boulevard, I watched all the girls and women who were walking past. We each did our best to be the boldest.

'Beautiful body,' said Dinu, with the tone of an established expert.

'I don't like her legs, retorted Robert, disdainfully.

In the twilight Dinu blushed; predictably he ignored my attempt at arbitration.

'Have you seen Sylvia lately?' countered Robert. The lovely Sylvia was a former 'sweetheart' of Dinu's, who he saw at the same family gatherings twice a year: on the Feast of Saint Dumitru and the third day of Easter. For several months, Sylvia has been under Robert's spell.

Dinu pretended to find their romance amusing.

'She's become quite ghastly recently.'

'You think so? Robert asked, disingenuously.

'But then, Sylvia's always been such a common girl...'

Seeing there was going to be a blazing row, I put an end to this dissection of Sylvia by asking a stupid question. After which I decided we should have a rest.

'Why don't we pick up some girls?'

I found the suggestion distasteful, and Robert sat down, happy that I hadn't agreed.

Dinu smoked dreamily. Robert was building up to give a great sigh. I just waited. I knew what was going to happen. We were seventeen years old, it was a summer night with military music playing in the background, so I knew the pair of them would soon become melancholy. Their rivalry would disappear. And then would come the vapid, whispered, tearful confessions between defenceless, all-too susceptible friends.

Dinu is more reserved when it comes to opening his heart. Robert, by contrast, is effusive and obsessive. His eyes close. He becomes distant, his imagination begins to wander. He sees himself as a tortured, demoniacal soul. Dinu is more modest; he says that he's like Anatole France: a sceptic and an epicurean.

But that particular night I was determined to put a stop to any conversation that looked like turning into a confessional. Robert avoided my gaze.

'You're so unhappy, doctor...'

The idea that we were going to talk about me was flattering. This is something that we all want, so we try and keep the conversation going for as long as possible. But at this moment in particular it was quite dangerous.

'I'm not the least bit unhappy...'

'It's pointless trying to hide it', replied Robert, his tone profound and lyrical.

Dinu was listening, waiting to get his revenge.

'How can you live without love, without women, without romance?' Robert went on, his eyes fixed on the top of a linden tree.

'That's how life is for me', I replied, humbly.'

'You call that living, young fellow?...'

When Robert speaks of life and 'love,' he speaks rhythmically, like an actor on stage.

'How can you not know the pleasures of youth... the pleasure of conquering a woman, having her at your feet, of thrusting aside the overflowing cup of love she offers you?...'

'What cup?' I pretended I didn't understand, foreseeing the danger of listening to Robert wax lyrical for a quarter of an hour.

'What? You don't understand me, doctor?'

'If you spoke a little more clearly...'

'To be inebriated by the scent of soft, smooth bodies, to walk under the trees, arm in arm with your slave...'

I glanced at Dinu, wondering why he didn't attack. In the grip of romantic fever, Robert had exposed himself. It was the ideal moment for Dinu's 'irony' to be aroused.

'Women... no one really understands them... to lie in pure white, virginal beds...'

Dinu couldn't contain himself.

'Come off it, Robert! How much longer do we have to put up with your fantasies?'

'They're not fantasies, my dear fellow', replied Robert, conceitedly. 'They are the realest of realities.'

'And when have you ever had a virgin?'

'I didn't say that I've had a virgin. I said "virginal beds"...'

'What do you mean by virginal?' I put in, adding fuel to the fire.

'Spare me your philology, doctor...'

'It's not a question of philology', I retorted, becoming angry. 'It's a question of virgins.'

Robert was upset that we didn't understand him. Whenever he can't come up with an answer, he sighs: we just don't understand him.

'Did you know that Maria wrote to me?...

Dinu and I were both certain that she hadn't.

'What did she say?'

'She bores me with her declarations of love.'

'I told her that I didn't love her anymore. She's not my *type*...'

And he lay down on the bench again, his gaze still fastened on the linden tree. He was thinking. By now the music had stopped. Couples came walking past under the trees, and Dinu watched them. Ah, the first days of summer and all their temptations! It filled me with excitement too, but I resisted. I didn't want to succumb to melancholy and end up telling them about my own more or less imaginary bucolic idylls.

'I've never seen you walking down the street with a woman', Dinu launched a surprise attack.

'I don't wander the streets with my *lovers*...'

There was a pause. I sensed that Dinu was getting agitated. He was certainly tempted to open his heart to someone. I've become extremely observant. I can quickly recognize people who are tormented by this inner compulsion. Many of my friends confide in me. They regard me as a born confessor. But they've never realized how little I care about the state of their souls. Because their confessions aren't sincere. They all try to be the most original in the eyes of others: to make them admire or sympathize with them.

Yet having said that, even I am occasionally tempted to bare my soul. But I hold myself back. I never tell anyone about what I imagine might be happening in the depths of my being. Confessions annoy me. They're a sign of weakness. I don't understand how a man could need support from someone else. When times are hard, even the best of friends is an enemy. At moments like that you have to be alone. It's alone that we either stand or fall.

And I can't confide in my friends. They have already made up their minds about me: I'm 'the doctor'. While I – from the little I understand – think otherwise. But if I were to open up to my friends, they'd tell me that everything I say is just a 'pose'. For boys, 'posing' means anything that distinguishes them from each other.

Bowing to the inevitable, I asked Dinu who his first woman had been.

'What, I haven't told you?' He sat up, absolutely delighted.

He had told me countless times.

'You told me ages ago, but I don't remember it that well. Besides, Robert should hear this as well...'

'Yes, yes, that would be interesting.'

As Robert sat up, I noticed that his eyes were alert.

I had heard about this escapade numerous times, in several different versions. So far, Dinu had had seventeen women. I even knew their names, the colour of their hair, and many other details. But his versions about the first woman interested me particularly – mainly because they were so varied and amusing. In one he told me that his first woman had been a widow with red hair who lived on the same street as him; in another, it was the opposite: she had raven-black hair, was married and very rich. But that wasn't all. He would recount sub-categories of the same story as well as variations of variations. For instance, his first woman had had black hair, was a widow and lived on the same street as him; or she was a redhead, married and rich; or lived on the same street, etc.

Dinu began in a nonchalant tone. He – a handsome boy in the Third Form, with black eyes, cherry lips, and wearing a well-tailored tunic – was walking home from school one day when, without warning, a flustered maidservant rushed out of an alleyway and grabbed him by the hand. Before he knew what was happening he found himself in a bedroom. In the bedroom there was a bed, and in the bed, a voluptuously clad girl with copper-coloured hair.

'A girl?' said Robert, his curiosity aroused.

'That was only how it seemed,' replied the other, warily.

I didn't say a word. But Robert decided to, and leant over to me.

'Doesn't it seem to you, Doctor, that Dinu's escapade is somewhat reminiscent of Caragiale's *The Sin*?

To me it certainly did seem 'reminiscent'. But feigning innocence, I replied: 'So you think Dinu's first woman was in Caragiale's play, *The Sin*?'

For the next five minutes we listened to military music coming from the other side of the lake.

'Have you read *The Sin*? Robert asked him.

'I don't remember...'

By the time we left the Cişmigiu Gardens it was getting late. As I write, I can't hear a single electric tram out on the boulevard. I don't feel like sleeping. It's hot. And I'm not at all happy.

I know what I'm going through: I'm sentimental. It's pointless trying to hide it. I'm as sentimental as any other adolescent. Otherwise I wouldn't be unhappy now. I have no reason to be unhappy.

So I understand now why I'm unhappy. It's because I didn't 'open my heart' to my friends. I'm just like all the others.

I need friends as well. There's no point in lying to myself. So I'm just like all the others.

I want truth, and nothing but the truth. I want to be sincere.

Yet apparently I'm not aware of this. Aren't I aware that I'm sentimental and weak, completely lacking willpower? Don't I also dream of blonde virgins, with whom I stroll through the park in the moonlight, or sail on the lake in a white rowing boat? Don't I imagine myself performing heroic deeds, winning the victor's laurels and the kisses of beautiful women who I've never met and who...?

But all these things are sad and foolish. I won't get any better by writing about them in my notebook. And I can't even write about them. They're laughable.

I must do something else. I should get my rope and whip myself. Because I'm an imbecile. Because I waste time wandering round the Cişmigiu Gardens, and am wasting time even now, dreaming of radiant marguerites with my eyes raised heavenward and my hands clasped over my breast.

And there's more. I'm the biggest simpleton of all, as much as I try to hide it. I'm such a simpleton that I'm not shocked at how I've wasted this whole evening, or at the feebleness of my soul, or the ruin that is my willpower, or the barren wasteland of my mind. And here I am, writing this instead of purifying myself with my whip. I'm disgusted with everything, even with pain. I was looking forward to physical pain. But now...

I'm not even tired. And I can't even read.

Which is a sure sign that I'm an imbecile.

A Friend

My friend Marcu is tall and skinny, with large, bulging eyes, curly hair, long fingers and long legs. He sits at the back of the class and reads French novels. The other boys think he's stupid, and they call him, 'Splinter' because of the length of his nose, and sometimes 'Moses' because he's a Jew. Marcu doesn't get annoyed at either of these nicknames. He arrives every morning with a novel in his bag, and sits quietly reading it at the back. If there's any commotion he just frowns and carries on reading. If people climb onto the desks, he puts his fingers in his ears and keeps reading. Even if a fight breaks out at the desk next to him, he simply moves to another desk and continues to read.

He reads his novel.

He even reads when a master is in the room. At these times he props his book against the back of the boy in front of him. He even reads while the master is actually teaching, because Marcu believes that schoolmasters are without exception blithering idiots, and that what they teach is harmful to a healthy brain. Sometimes his neighbours warn him: 'Marcu, he's nearly got to you!'

This means that those whose names come just before his in the class register have already been called. Disgruntled, Marcu raises his large eyes from his book. He inquires about the lesson. Occasionally he even goes so far as to ask someone to explain something. He never misses an opportunity to throw the master a 'red herring' – as long as he doesn't have to spend too long up at the blackboard, because the novel must be read at all costs. But if he's asked a question in chemistry, however, he doesn't move a muscle. He knows he'll still get an 'Unsatisfactory' anyway.

'Ionescu Corneliu, Ionescu Stelian, Malareanu Marcu...'

A classmate nudged him: 'Up you go, Marcu! Your name's been called.'

Marcu joined the queue in front of the blackboard, arms crossed. When his turn came, and Toivinovici asked him a question, he calmly answered: 'I don't know sir.'

'What about the industrial preparation of sulphuric acid?'

'I don't know sir.'

So Toivinovici asked the first two boys, who had been cramming frantically all week.

They gabbled away and covered the board with formulae.

'That'll do. Marcu, could you draw a diagram of the structure of the compound pentaphosphoric acid?'

'I don't know sir.'

'Go and sit down, Marcu.'

He walked away, grinning, his long arms bumping against the desks. When he got back to his seat, he complained to his neighbours: 'Why did you make me close my book?'

Once Noisil caught him reading in class. The master was pacing up and down the room, explaining the different phases of the Hundred Years War, when he spotted Marcu immersed in volume I of *Le Rouge et le Noir*, which I had lent him.

Noisil promptly put his hand on his shoulder.

'Reading books in history class is not allowed. What did I tell you before?'

Marcu couldn't remember. Noisil suspended him for three days.

'You are to donate the book to the school library,' Noisil told him.

Filled with chagrin, I remembered that it was my book.

When he came back to school, Marcu told us that his parents hadn't found out about him being suspended, because every morning he left home with his schoolbag and spent the day reading novels in the Cişmigiu Gardens, until the factory sirens sounded in the evening.

'God bless Noisil!' he said. 'Thanks to him I was able to finish *Les Miserables*.'*

He always cheats during tests. He either gets out his textbook or a crib sheet, or his neighbours whisper the answers to him. Nothing seems to ruffle him, and he never spares a thought for what would happen if he were unlucky enough to get caught. The masters think he's dense and uneducated. When he's called up to the blackboard, he goes red and comes out with irrelevant nonsense, stutters or doesn't say anything at all. This is why his classmates consider him incurably stupid. Although some people, those who are less inclined to judge hastily, wonder why someone who reads so many books is sent out of class so often, and either mumbles to himself, or says nothing at all like a complete ignoramus.

'Because he doesn't care about school or the teachers!' I cry, taking his side.

I know that when he's not forced to regurgitate schoolwork, Marcu speaks beautifully and with great originality. We became friends one evening as we walked home from school together. I was criticizing *La Garçonne**, a novel by Margueritte, while he defended it.

Up till then I hadn't known any more about him than all the others. But I soon realized that I was wrong. He was crazy about Balzac, and even managed to convert me. We read only Balzac, everything we could lay our hands on. We were soon great authorities on *La Comédie Humaine*, and competed with each other to know the most about the characters, minutiae and all the other curiosities of Balzac's work. When our supplies ran out, we scoured the bookshops and second-hand dealers until we found what we wanted.

Between us we introduced the rest of the class to Balzac. One of our first disciples was Robert. We tormented him by giving him the worst novels to read, and he admired them. When he began to suspect that we were making fun of him, he would assure us hesitantly: 'To be honest I didn't think *L'Enfant Maudit** was brilliant. It's good, but not very...'

The other boys call Marcu a communist and an anarchist, but it doesn't bother him, because it's his own fault that they use these names. One morning, he came to school with some socialist propaganda material, booklets by Engels and Kautsky, and Marx's *Das Kapital*. Another time he took two French books with red covers out of his bag: Stirner's *L'Unique**, and a large volume by Kropotkin.

Marcu said they were very interesting, but the others – who knew all about him – discovered that the books were anarchistic, and began to be frightened of him. They don't hate him, but look down on him, and some speak with aristocratic disdain of the danger of the 'Bolshevik hell.'

Marcu was never really serious when he said he supported anarchism. He simply said that it was interesting, and if we asked he would explain anarchist ideology to us. But if he felt like annoying the aristocrats, he would admit to being a disciple of Kropotikin and Bakunin.

The aristocrats are convinced that he really is a follower of anarchism and communism, but that he's afraid to admit it publicly. If anyone were to tell the aristocrats that anarchists and communists are irreconcilable, they would say he was talking nonsense.

Marcu assures the sons of the gentry that it won't be long before their land is expropriated again. When I asked him how he knew this, he told me he made it up, to worry the landowners' sons. In our class there are only two, but Marcu claims that there are actually far more.

Not everyone knows how to talk to Marcu. He always finds a reason to doubt whatever he has just said. This doesn't bother me at all; on the contrary, I find him most original. Only when I produce one argument after another and he still won't accept them as valid – because he finds them dubious – do I get angry. I think he actually enjoys all this, and maybe I'm not far wrong in guessing that the aim of all his arguing is just to annoy the rest of us.

'I've got him going!'

Whenever he manages to 'get someone going', Marcu is very pleased with himself. He runs his fingers through his curly hair and can't sit still. That's why not just anyone can talk to him.

Whenever there's a general discussion in class and the aristocrats are involved, he automatically takes the other side, even if it's wrong. He always ends up 'getting the aristocrats going'.

Particularly Furtuneanu. Furtuneanu refers to him as a 'destructive Jew,' forgetting that he's actually very close to another Jew, Lazimir, a rich boy with whom he plays poker every week. Furtuneanu has loathed Marcu ever since he was 'discourteous' to him. We all had to have our hair cut, shaved to at least number 3, and most of us did as we were told. The few who forgot were sent to get it done during class, to their great delight. Furtuneanu was the only one to come back with his dark, flowing locks still intact, untouched by clippers for two years. His father came with him, and told the Headmaster that if his son were forced to have his hair cut then he would remove him from the school. The Headmaster gave in, and accepted the 'medical certificate' that explained that the pupil Furtuneanu Petre couldn't have a hair cut because he suffered from an ear infection. It was true that Furtuneanu had had otitis, but that was a year ago and he still had long hair. The rest of the class rebelled at first, but then gave in, just like the Headmaster.

However, the other masters demanded an explanation. So Furtuneanu provided one: 'After suffering from an ear infection I now catch cold easily. If my head were shaved, it would only take the slightest breeze and the infection would come back. That's why...'

'...His mummy keeps him wrapped in cotton wool,' Marcu whispered to the boy next to him, but loud enough for Trollo to hear. The others all sniggered.

'Please don't address me in a way in which I wouldn't address you. Please behave with decorum. Please make an effort to be well-mannered, even if that's not the way you've been brought up at home...'

'It sounds like you're going to choke', Marcu replied, impassively.

The roars of laughter prevented Furtuneanu from saying any more. But after the lesson had finished, he went and sat next to Marcu and talked to him for a quarter of an hour. His face turned bright red, and he kept spraying saliva through a gap where two of his front teeth had fallen out. He insulted Marcu, told him he was badly brought-up, and concluded with these terrible words: 'Don't ever shake my hand in the street again!'

Marcu was red in the face as well, but seemed unperturbed. Later on he told me how glad he was to have been able to make Furtureanu spit and bellow for a quarter of an hour.

From that moment on, Furtuneanu became Marcu's sworn enemy.

He had no reason to admire him in any case, because he didn't really know him. During lessons, in front of the master and his classmates, Marcu rarely says anything original. Only in our private discussions is he able to be himself. Perhaps he's nervous in front of the other boys, or thinks it's wiser not to reveal himself too much. All the same, I was astonished when, quite inexplicably, Marcu wasn't able to analyse Eminescu's poem, the *Emperor and Proletarian* without referring to the criticism by Gherea. Yet this wasn't the first time that he couldn't answer a question in class without relying on other people's work. Perhaps he finds the presence of the class and the master intimidating.

Marcu told me that he doesn't believe in anything, and doubts everything. Yet when he's defending a theory or opposing someone, he will only challenge – and with great precision – the actual arguments that they put forward. And when it comes to his own assertions, he makes his case with great conviction. Perhaps he doesn't realize that at these times he isn't being very sceptical.

*

Today I read a book by Ionel Teodoreanu, *Childhood Lane*, and I cried. I wasn't ashamed: I cried. I quickly washed my face with cold water so no one would see an emotional, short-sighted boy with tears in his eyes. All day long I was in love with Sonia. I even believed I'd had more success with her than Stefănel did. I imagined that I was handsome, interesting, and illustrious. I imagined myself at la Medeleni, playing *Scheherezade*, with Sonia near me.

It's true that, this morning, two more spots appeared on my face. I studied them in the mirror for a long time, and wondered if Sonia would like me. So I asked her. And Sonia replied that she was more impressed by my genius than by the number of spots on my forehead...

There's no point pretending: I'm unhappy. I've never been to the 'country.' And when spring sunlight streams through the open windows of my attic, I dream of orchards and blossom-laden branches, springs, luxuriant bowers, young maidens and romantic idylls during the Easter holidays. Even though I've never been to the country.

On summer evenings I roam the streets, stroll under the acacia trees and dream of rustic love affairs, avowals in the moonlight, or passionate words that I'll never utter. On summer evenings it's pointless to try and finish a chapter of *Felix le Dantec*. My heart has undergone a change, and I blow out the lamp and begin to dream. Many, many times I've wondered what comes over me on summer evenings. But I've never found the answer.

And today I read *Childhood Lane*, and cried. I cried because I've never experienced the same emotions as the heroes in this book. I've only ever dreamt about them. I've never had a country estate and I've never had girlfriends who come there to convalesce. When I was small I used to go to sleep shivering with cold, and played with the bootmaker's daughters from next door, who never owned a pair of stockings and wore calico dresses. I've only ever dreamt of young ladies, while still playing with the bootmaker's daughters.

So I cried, and then I put the book back on the shelf and laughed. I laughed at myself, because I was still a sentimental dreamer. I said to myself: *Childhood Lane* is a praline for faint-hearted mummy's boys like Robert and Dinu. It's a book full of expensive dolls, with posed pictures and idyllic romance. It's a book for boyars' sons, who ride horses, smoke, and kiss the apricot blossom.

I've never kissed apricot blossom. But I've bitten my lip because I don't know who I am. I've asked myself a thousand questions and tortured myself to find the answers, and I've wasted away because I was unable to find them.

I've felt my flesh quiver, and whipped myself because we were poor and couldn't do what other people did.

Have I forgotten all of this? Have I forgotten my novel? Have I forgotten my soul, which suffers unbeknown to anyone, my mind that struggles on, yearning for things that the idiots around me have never even heard of?

Did I cry because a rich, handsome adolescent with chestnut hair fell in love with a boyar's daughter who enjoys smoking and plays

Scheherezade on the piano? Did I see my own generation reflected in the happy young people at Medeleni? Did I waste my holidays thinking about Sonia's eyes, or did I spend my summer in rooms full of old papers, my myopic eyes watering, my body tormented by the sap of adolescence, my soul feverish from waiting for a truth I had been seeking day and night?

Where was my decision to show myself to the world as I really am, conscious of my superiority and the foolishness of my contemporaries? Where was the brute desire to find and possess myself entirely, if I cry because Stefănel lived out 'the very last fairytale?'

Had I forgotten that I was clenching my teeth in envious rage, that I had sworn an oath to myself that I would soon become someone? And that then I'd savagely force apart the thighs of the most beautiful women, simply because I, *I*, had endured years and years of the torments of the flesh, because *I* had never had any money, or a beautiful body, or beautiful eyes, or a beautiful face?

Had I forgotten that I cried on the pages of a book from the National Collection of Culture? That I finished *Childhood Lane* before I read Dantec's *Lute universelle*?*

Aren't I ashamed of myself? Aren't I ashamed of my name and my yearnings, my desires?...

All in vain. I'm still just as unhappy and just as much in love with Sonia.

Forgive me, Ionel Teodoreanu; but if Sonia really exists, then tell her that an ugly boy who doesn't know what he wants is sad because of her eyes.

Tell her to come and give me the gift of three consoling words.

Tell her that I ask nothing more of her than she comfort me, and that she won't be horrified at the sight of me.

But if Sonia doesn't want to leave where she is, leave her Moldova, tell her to send me her address, and then I'll sell all my Felix Le Dantec books and come and find her, so that Sonia can comfort me...

VI

Monday 8am – 9am:

German Class

In my first year I had to retake French, German, and Romanian. I spent my afternoons on a piece of waste ground, barefoot, sweating and myopic, playing *oină*[5]. I was renowned for the speed with which I caught the ball and hurled it at the knees of the players in the square zone. There was even talk of me being selected for the school team. Two things were against me, however. The first was that I was one of the laziest, most careless and badly behaved members of the class. And then I was short-sighted. Even if I could see the opponents' knees very clearly, I would never be able to see the ball in time when I was in the square. I only got away with it because of the lack of skill of the person throwing the ball.

Three retakes almost certainly meant I would have to repeat a year. When I heard the news I thought seriously about suicide for a quarter of an hour. It's true that the idea of torture and death terrifies me. But because I could only save face by performing a courageous act, I wracked my brains to try to create a scenario where my friends would find me at the very last moment, when I was about to swallow the pill. I wasn't sure how to get a hold of such a pill, the kind that people who are depressed use to kill themselves, but this didn't interfere with my plans. I imagined myself at the height of despair, the pill between my teeth, fighting off my friends who were trying to save my life. I could almost hear my cries as I struggled with them: 'No, no... let me die!...'

By the time I reached this point I was in a highly emotional state. Driven by some obscure desire, I let my thoughts run on.

I imagined myself dead. I saw my astonished friends, the class-mates who were secretly delighted at this unexpected event, heard my mother sobbing. As I pictured all this I wept, because I felt I was being victimized by Faradopol, our German master, a portly man who was a major in the Army Reserve. At my graveside, the other boys cried out: 'He's a criminal, a criminal!...'

And I regretted that, since I was dead, I couldn't smile to show them my gratification.

After a quarter of an hour, however, I suddenly calmed down. I sat on a bench and watched the crowds of happy people who were thronging the boulevard.

'They don't have to retake German', I said to myself, becoming wretched again.

German filled me with horror. At first I had considered it my patriotic duty to not study the language of my enemies. But then I began to be afraid of the master. He hadn't got the job of Head-master. He had returned from the front as an officer, and a mere glance from him could immediately make us forget our 'lesson'.

'Was haben sie heute?'

For six whole years, this opening remark had terrified me. As I sit in the front row, I'm almost always the first to have to answer.

'Das Haus!'

'Jackass! What sort of answer is that?'

'?...'

'You must reply using a proper sentence. How many times do I have to tell you?'

'Was haben sie heute?'

'Haben sie heute: das Haus!'

'How must you reply?'

'...using a proper sentence', I mumbled.

What with all these sentences, plus the looks and the corpulence of the German master, I forgot everything.

'Let's move on. Where's your exercise book?'

In my exercise book – in 'German' letters – I had copied out several dozen words that we were meant to learn.

'Road?'

'*Weg!*'
'Article?'
'*Der Weg?*'
'*Das!*... Jackass!'
'Ornament?'
'*Sch...raf?*'
'What do you mean, *Schraf*? Ornament!'
'I know that it starts with '*Sch*', I said, trying to placate him.
So he gave me a clue: '*Sch... Schm... Schm...*'
'*Schumf?*' I said, hesitantly.
'*Der Schmuk!* Jackass!'
'To know?'
'*Wissen.*'
'Conjugate it.'
'*Wissen, wust, gewusten.*'
'And how do we get the passive subjunctive, third person plural?'
'?'
'Go and sit down. You get three...'

＊

I got up from my desk and made my way home.

My mother already knew. Five of her friends had told her the news, assuring her that I'd move up a class in the autumn. The storm wasn't easily weathered. I defended myself by saying that I was being 'persecuted.'

'But why is it only you who gets persecuted?'

'I don't know... that's just how it is. They want to persecute me.'

We agreed between us that I would divide my summer holidays in two: up till August I would be free, after that I would work with a tutor.

The tutor was the son of a Jewish tailor, and was called Sami. He was only sixteen, still played marbles and read Nick Winter, but he studied at the evangelical school and was having violin lessons at the Conservatoire.

'How's it going, young man?'

'Listen, Sami: we're not going to work today. Mama is going to see my grandmother. Let's have an ice cream instead.'

'Have you got any money?'

'Tell Mama that I need an exercise book.'

'That still only leaves me with twenty bani[6]...'

'Never mind, I'll give you some stamps.'

'How much should I tell your mother an exercise book costs?'

'Fifty bani.'

'And if she won't give it to me?'

Sami was as mistrustful as he was shrewd. He took all my marbles, and made me promise to go through all the clothes that belonged to the German who was billeted with us and take any unused stamps. When our sessions began, since Mama sat in, Sami would pretend to be strict: 'Now, young man, *Cherman* is difficult. I have already told your mother this...'

By September I still hadn't learned a thing. But by then all the Germans had left, and the Minister of Education no longer required pupils to learn German in the first year at the lycée. I had escaped.

But ever since then, German has haunted me.

*

The German master is now the Headmaster. His face is even more severe than ever, his voice rings out forbiddingly every morning, and when he gets angry he hits the pupils.

'Why are you late?'

Satchel on his back, the boy stood in the doorway, petrified.

'I was just...'

'Get a move on, lummox!'

I am the only 'jackass' in the class, and he has only hit me the once. I had left my umbrella in the classroom, and went back to get it. But as all the doors were locked, I climbed in through the window. Then I heard the Headmaster's threatening footsteps approaching. I hid behind the door

'What on earth are you doing here?'

'...umbrella...'

'The final bell has rung. Why haven't you left?'

'I did leave. But I came back.'

The Headmaster's eyes flashed.

'And... how did you get in?'

The question echoed in my ears like a trumpet blast. I wasn't brave or strong enough to reply. I forgot who I was and what I was doing in this classroom with a Headmaster and an umbrella.

Suddenly I felt my head being shaken three times to the right then three times to the left. My cheeks flushed bright red from shame and the stinging pain. My eyes filled with tears. I was trembling, just like my umbrella.

'Get out of here, you jackass!'

But I didn't have anywhere to go. I backed into the stove, almost in a trance.

'You'll scorch your clothes, you nincompoop!'

I thanked him for the advice, moist-eyed and humble.

But I still didn't learn any German.

All this year I've infuriated the master.

'I'm sorry, sir, but I left my exercise book at home...'

'One...'

I was glad that at least he hadn't tormented me at the blackboard. When he did call my name, however, I would stiffen, turn pale and grasp my exercise book and textbook.

'*Was haben sie heute?*'

Naturally, I had no choice but to answer. To give the impression that I had been studying hard, I gabbled the words.

'*Lebens Gote.*'

'Not Gote. *Goethe...*'

But I never knew the answer. And after a longer or shorter interval, I always ended up with an 'Unsatisfactory'.

*

Every Monday morning, in a febrile state, I pace up and down between the rows of desks thinking about Ibsen's *Brand*. He gives me courage. I frown and imagine that I'm Brand, braving the storm. Brand was misunderstood, in the same way that my German master doesn't understand me. We're similar. Perhaps we have the same soul. As I walk back and forth among the desks I am keenly aware of this.

But when there's a lot of noise in the classroom, I'm unable to think about Brand. I press my fists against my forehead, but never manage to summon up his image. All I see is mountains covered in snow. Brand never appears. And then I start to tremble, my heart aches, and I become nervous and agitated, rather like Fănică does in Chemistry. No one realizes this, but when Brand doesn't appear it's extremely difficult for me. So at these moments I get on with learning German vocabulary.

All things considered, the Headmaster isn't really a bad man. Towards the end of the year, he summons all those who are in danger of failing to the staff common room for a 'reckoning'. It's warm in the room, and he's smoking a cigarette.

'So: what do you know?'

'Schiller.'

'You know Schiller?'

We all smile, because everyone has to smile when the Headmaster tells a joke.

'Really? You know about Schiller?'

We realize that our smiles haven't had the desired effect. Someone laughs. Others fiddle with their handkerchiefs, and the Headmaster seems satisfied. Cautiously, I nudge the boys either side of me. The laughter has to stop, because the Headmaster is looking serious again. If we laugh too much, he'll get in a bad mood.

'Let's do a little test...'

For once he doesn't get angry. He listens as we read and translate from our abridged textbooks, but all the time his thoughts are on Prahova county.

An hour and fifteen cigarettes later, the Headmaster gives us all a 'Satisfactory'.

'Jackasses!... Off you go then!'

VII

The Retake

School has finished.

And I'm sure I'll have to retake maths. I failed because I wanted to; or to be more precise, I didn't pass because I didn't want to.

I'm not ashamed. I've known for some time that I completely lack willpower. It's probably only my naïve classmates who imagine that I'm determined because I read erudite books late into the night.

I just told them that I like reading; I don't force myself to do it. But they refused to listen.

Naturally, everything went as expected. During our final lesson, Vanciu told us: 'Those of you who wish to improve your marks can come into school in three days time, at two o'clock in the afternoon. It will be possible to improve my marks, because I'll be asking questions on subjects covered in every term'

I had got an 'Unsatisfactory' every term. I stood on a desk and shouted: 'Well lads, there'll be *no sleep* tonight!'

And I told anyone who would listen: 'I'm going to start revising at two o'clock this afternoon. I'll work till ten. I'll eat, then get some kip, and then get up at two in the morning. I'll work through till tomorrow morning and then repeat the process twice more. Today I'll finish Trigonometry, until lunchtime tomorrow I'll revise algebra, Newton's binomial and Pascal's triangle. After lunch I'll finish algebra. The day after tomorrow I'll do the same. And the day after that I'll walk away from the blackboard top of the class and astonish Vanciu. In these three days I'll learn everything I've haven't learnt during the year and then I'm free... After that I'll go to bed and sleep for forty hours straight off, like Champollion when he had managed to decipher hieroglyphics...'

I was full of enthusiasm, and believed what I was saying. When the enthusiasm wore off, however, I began to have my doubts. But I forced myself to preserve this enthusiasm because I really needed it.

When I got home I told my family what I had decided to do: 'Until tomorrow I'm going to revise trigonometry for all it's worth.'

After supper I went up to the attic. It was hot, and I was sleepy. I thought: 'I can't start maths straight away. First I need to get my brain into training. For about an hour I'll read a book that has nothing to do with Newton's binomial or Pascal's triangle.

'Right then,' I said out loud when I saw that it was three in the morning: 'Paper, pencil, logarithm tables, trigonometry textbook.'

I carefully cleared the table of anything that might distract me: a book by August Comte, volume III of *The History of Roman Literature* by Iorga, *Sanctuaires d'Orient** by Schuré, reviews and pamphlets. Then I laid out everything that I would need.

'The first few lessons aren't difficult at all,' I said under my breath, to bolster my courage. 'So let's start with trigonometric lines: *the sine and cosine.*'

But then I started reading the preface, in which Mr Tutuc quoted a passage by Mr Bianu. In this passage the author claimed that, as intelligent as his dull-witted maths teachers may have considered him, he found Spiru Haret's book on trigonometry quite delightful.

'Trigonometry must be extremely interesting,' I thought, without much conviction.

But every time I tried to read the first chapter, I either found that my pencil wasn't sharp enough, or that my logarithmic tables weren't easy to grasp. Or that the window squeaked, my legs weren't in the right position, my shirt collar was uncomfortable, the paper covering the desk was stained, my icon hadn't been dusted since Thomas Sunday, the ink in the inkwell had dried up, or that I didn't have enough paper, etc.

The clock struck half past three.

'Get on with it!' I reprimanded myself.

And I drew a circle, divided it into four, and at the end of each diameter I put a capital letter: A, B, C, D. I imagined a thirty-five degree arc then joined the most extreme point of that arc to the centre of the circle. But I saw that I had produced a forty-five degree arc.

'That's no good!' I said, glad to have to draw another circle. 'This is an eighth of a circle and its sine is $3/\sqrt{-2}$, while its cosine is $2/\sqrt{3}$.

I crossed out the circle with the forty-five degree arc and drew another one next to it, with an arc of only thirty-five degrees. But when I was about to dissect it with two perpendicular diameters, the circle that I had crossed out suddenly caught my attention. I screwed up the sheet of paper and threw it out the window. The third circle was much better, and I gave it a commendable thirty-five degree arc. The arc was $ab = 35°$, and in the centre I put a O, because that's what always goes in the centre.

Next I read three pages without stopping. They were very well written and extremely clear, but it was hot in the attic, and I was thinking about how in a month's time I'd be in the forests of Sibiu.

By evening I had read twenty-seven pages, with a hundred and one to go. This was because at 4.30 I had taken a cold shower; at 5.30 I had decided I was starving and went downstairs to have something to eat; at 6.30 I started reading a magazine; at 7 o'clock I was thirsty, at 7.15 my pencil broke, at 7.30 the sound of the birds twittering made me feel melancholy, at 8 o'clock I felt persecuted, at 8.15 I lit the lamp, – even though it wasn't really necessary – at 8.30 I studied my face in the mirror, at 8.40 I made some notes for the psychological aspects of my novel, at 8.50 I decided to have a short rest so as not to overexert myself, and at 8.55 I was called to supper.

After supper I played the piano for quite a long time, something I hadn't done for several years. It was quarter past eleven when I went back up to the attic.

'Leave it,' I thought. 'I mustn't make my eyes tired by reading late at night. I'll set the alarm to wake me at three.'

Quite content, I began to get undressed. But wasn't three too early? So I decided to get up at four.

As I went over to the table to turn out the lamp, I changed my mind again and set the alarm for five.

And so at five o'clock it duly rang. But as I had had bad dreams all night, I just let it ring.

'Leave me in peace, will you', I said, still half asleep, as if it were the clock's fault for ringing at five. And I turned over and went back to sleep.

'Hey, you've got maths to do! Get out of bed!'

'So what if I've got maths to do? Was I made for maths, or was maths made for me?'

And I went back to sleep. But the morning sun touched my eyelids, and I woke up again. I began to regret sleeping for an hour and a half longer than I needed to, and cursed myself out loud: 'I'm just an adolescent like all the rest. I'll never amount to anything. I'm a good for nothing. What a shame I've wasted all this time in school. I've got as much willpower as an oven-ready chicken.'

All this was meant to shake me out of my indifference and make me fall in love with trigonometry.

In vain. Once I had washed and dressed I started reading a chapter in the book by Iorga.

'Am I really foolish enough to waste my energy on maths at six in the morning?'

In fact it wasn't six o'clock, but five to seven. I read *The History of Roman Literature* until eight, when my father brought me some milk and found me feverishly flicking through my logarithmic tables. He looked very pleased.

'How's it going?'

'It's difficult, very difficult. I've been working at it since four in the morning. I don't know what to do. I'm awfully tired.'

My father looked at me fondly.

'Go out into the garden for a while, and then do some more work. I don't think it'll be all that bad, the questions won't be too hard...'

'He said he would ask us some difficult questions...'

At quarter-past eight I counted how many pages I still had to read, and divided them up among the hours that I had left.

I did the calculation three times, because it seemed to be important to have an exact answer.

I drew a circle.

'What if I don't turn up for the exam?'

'Then I'll fail.'

'So what if I fail?'

'Everyone will make fun of me.'

'So what if everyone makes fun of me?'

My mind was made up, so I stopped dividing the circle into four equal parts and marking the extremities of the diameters A, B, C, D.

'What's it to me if I fail? Don't I know who I am? Aren't I still myself?'

I was right: I was still myself. But that was of no significance to Vanciu.

'Why should I care about Vanciu?'

That was right too: why should I care about Vanciu?

'It would actually be better if I fail. I'll have plenty of time to study hard during the summer. I'll work for four hours a day, so that even Vanciu will be amazed. And then he won't fail me next year, or in my final year either. But I'll have to make a serious effort to understand maths once and for all. I'll study all this summer. It's a really wise decision on my part: to study over the summer...'

Filled with delight, I picked up my books and stacked them under the table that was covered with magazines. Then I hurried downstairs and told everyone that I wasn't going to the exam.

'What? You want me to just scrape through? And then next year I'll fail again, and again in my final year?'

I'll have to make a serious effort to understand maths once and for all. During the summer I'll have plenty of time. It's the wisest thing to do...'

Because after all, this year I'm going to fail, just like in all the other years.

It was only to be expected. In fact I'd predicted it would happen as long ago as last winter, although I had never told anyone.

Prize-giving

This morning, rows of benches were set out in the schoolyard, along with a lectern, a few chairs and a table on which were piled the books that would be presented to the prize-winners. The boys, dressed for the occasion, stood around in groups, while the girls were more serious and impatient, their faces glowing. One or two people sidled up to the table to steal a surreptitious glance at the books, which had the prize-winners' names written on the covers. Then they went back to the others, and the news spread rapidly along the benches. One of the winners blushed, pretending not to believe it.

'Don't take any notice... he's lying!' Although he actually thought he had won first prize..

The boys in their final year were wearing straw hats, and obviously felt obliged to laugh and mock. With an air of condescension they used the informal form of 'you' when speaking to the younger boys. Then, along with everyone else, they turned their attention to the preparations going on at the lectern, the table with all the books, and made comments about the masters' faces. 'The Dragon,' the hairy school servant, bowed his head so he could hear the Headmaster's orders. A secretary brought a sheet of paper on which the prize-winners' names were written in alphabetical order. One or two parents came and sat nervously in the front row, waving and smiling to the masters.

The pupils from the Remove and Fifth Form laughed loudly at all the jokes made by the Sixth-Formers, secretly hoping to become part of their cliques. They gathered round them, hanging on their every word. When the older boys deigned to speak to them, they were thrilled. Some were lucky enough to be asked their opinion, while others were even allowed to join in the conversation. But these were the privileged few. This friendship with 'the big boys' was undoubtedly due to many 'favours' provided in the school tuck shop, at the tavern on the corner or by running errands for them. Others had established similar relationships by having secret card games late into the night, often after midnight.

At ten thirty the 'festivities' began. Standing at the lectern, the Headmaster gave a speech. He made special mention of 'the school's activities, the percentage of pupils who had passed their exams, and those who had won prizes', and concluded with exhortations to excel.

'...at our lycée, ladies and gentlemen, the pupil's work, his diligence, his intelligence and perseverance – or, put another way – the diligent and intelligent pupil who has not wasted his time, who has made full use of the enlightenment that is so generously provided by our school, the diligence of this pupil, of which there are many in this school, has been rewarded. Therefore we can say, ladies and gentlemen, that after this, the seventh year of our school's existence, after many achievements and rewards...'

The boys sitting on the benches at the back laughed and clapped. Every now and then, masters would turn round and glare at them. When the Headmaster had sat down, the Director of Music began looking for the boys who played in the ensemble. He could only find nine.

'Mr Boloveanu?' said the Headmaster, looking at him impatiently.

The Director of Music was beside himself.

'Hurry up, gentlemen, for goodness sake! Where's the bass drum? How many alto trumpeters are there?'

I was one of the alto trumpeters. But after every rehearsal my lips were swollen and I had trouble breathing. It was this that had dissuaded me from going to rehearsals for the past two months. I hid under the bench so he couldn't see me.

The Director of Music – a corpulent visionary – took up his baton and began. 'The March' was one of his numerous compositions. But without enough trombonists, and with a feeble drummer, the fanfare was uninspiring. The melody was inaudible in places, drowned out by the alto trumpets. To the Headmaster's vexation, the finales were almost always off-key. Eventually the Director of Music flew into a rage. When the symbol clashed a half-tone flat, he went over to the player and hit him with his baton.

'I shall report you to the Headmaster!'

Then he turned to the musicians.

'Why don't you ever come to rehearsals?... *Forte* over there, *forte*!'

The applause, which went on for far too long, made the Headmaster and the Director of Music blush.

'Play your *Medley*', suggested the Headmaster, imperiously.

The boys had been waiting for this great revelation with bated breath: the maestro's latest composition.

'Bravo! Bravo!...'

But a glance from the podium silenced them.

The parents grew restless. The prize-winners were bathed in perspiration.

'Ssh! On the count of four, you begin. One, two...'

'The National Medley' started with a *doinā*[7]. But the soloist, a tall, dark-haired, hollow-cheeked boy, was exhausted. When he had to hold a note for more than three beats, he puffed out his cheeks, went red in the face and closed his eyes. The tone flattened, and became a squeaking sound.

'Firănescu! Blow harder, lad!' the Director begged, gripping the baton.

A group of pupils who were sitting behind the ensemble took up the cry: 'Go for it, Firănescu!...'

When the *doinā* ended and the *sârba*[8] began, the soloist coughed and took a deep breath. The members of the ensemble smiled at the audience, the Director of Music smiled at the ensemble, and the audience tapped their feet in time with the music.

At the back, the elite pupils produced an accompaniment of their own, banging their fists on the desks. Parents turned to see what was going on. Then in the middle of the *sârba* the Headmaster stood up and roared: 'You at the back! I'll have you all thrown out...'

The amateur musicians fell silent, soon followed by the ensemble themselves, who were showered with applause. There was a five minute break, and then the prize-giving began. A secretary who spoke with a lisp called out the names: 'Brădescu, Mihail, Upper Sixth Science Class, first prize with honours.'

The ensemble played a triumphal arpeggio: *'Do-mi-sol-do. Do-sol-mi-dooo...Do-mi-sol-do...'*

'That'll do. Vasilica, Dumitru, Upper Sixth Science Class, second prize.'

'Bravo! Bravo, Dumitru!'

Vasilica Dumitru, a lanky lad with a stoop, droopy ears, a freckled face pockmarked by smallpox scars, with a red nose and narrow forehead, came up timidly to the prize-giving table, as befits a washwoman's son. The Director gave him an insipid smile, shook his hand then frowned and smoothed his hair. Other lucky, diligent pupils were then called up in turn. Each of them was given an armful of books, or sometimes only one, and then, blushing, they stumbled away, not daring to go back to their seats. They talked amongst themselves, comparing prizes, and from deep down inside us, jealously rose like red-hot steam. All the other pupils, an anonymous crowd of mediocrities who had just scraped through or had had to retake – no one who was repeating a year had come to the ceremony – greeted their successful classmates with disingenuous applause.

'Bravo, Mandea!'

'Live long and prosper!'

'Bravo, Sandu!'

They shook hands with Alexandru Alexandrescu, all the while thinking that, by rights, they too could have got a prize. Some looked gloomy, while others put on a show of excitement as they applauded their fellow pupils.

Although I was eager to hear everything that was said, I was afraid the others might find out what I was feeling deep down inside. I did my best to appear calm, so no one could accuse me of being jealous of a few dull-witted prize-winners. But as they gathered round me, I felt my resolve weaken. It wouldn't be long before I gave voice to my hatred. I hated these uncultured, characterless adolescents with broad foreheads who always did their homework, went to the cinema and masturbated every night. I hated their bodies whether they were puny or muscular, pale or swarthy, their rosy or pasty faces, their sunken, dark-ringed eyes. All my work, my torments and my results went unappreciated. Simply because I couldn't understand maths or speak German. My opinion was coloured by vehement feelings of injustice. All that was really necessary to me were the things I liked. What was I supposed to do with maths and natural science?

'I learn what I want to learn, do you hear me. We're all a bunch of idiots...'

And my conversation with a classmate who had won a prize came to an abrupt, savage end: 'Idiots, do you hear me?'

I was probably shouting, because people turned to look and my classmate moved away, rather intimidated.

Eventually I calmed down, by thinking about my books and manuscripts as well as this herd of adolescents. I had been exaggerating as usual, in order to console myself.

Dinu and I looked at the result sheets that had been pasted onto a window. Only four people from our class had failed maths: Dinu, Chioreanu, Bonaş and myself. Dinu was my friend. The other two were the worst in the class. This should have humiliated me. In the past, I had at least kept company with a better quality of failures...

I walked home with Dinu, laughing and joking.

As I walked into the dining room, I asked everyone: 'Do you know how many people in my class failed maths? Sixteen.'

Everyone was astonished. They looked at me sympathetically and tried to console me. Although I pretended to be upset, I was actually filled with joy that Papa didn't lecture me and Mama didn't stop my pocket money for a week. They asked me all about the prize-giving, about the masters, my friends, classmates, the people I knew and didn't know.

I had to pretend to be upset until evening.

Or perhaps I really was upset...

IX

The Summer Holidays

It's hot, and I can read whatever I like. I haven't given any thought to the retake. I'll worry about maths at the end of August, and then I'll do some work. I'm free, the master of my own time. I've been wondering if I shouldn't just leave, run away forever. It's a thought that keeps coming back insistently every time I manage to thrust it aside. My nights are tormented by it. It would be wonderful to run away... but maybe I just don't have the courage. I keep thinking of all the obstacles that I wouldn't know how to overcome. I don't understand anything about passports. If I could just get hold of one, it would be easy for me to work it out.

All my friends tell me that they've wanted to run away as well. But in my case, running away isn't just a passing desire for adventure, or a childish capitulation to the drudgery of school. I have to run away because of an inner necessity that I don't understand, but which has seized control of my will. Otherwise I feel that it will tear my soul apart, that I'll suffocate. I feel the need to live the way I want, to struggle.

Up here in the attic, the only thing I struggle with is myself. I've become a tried and tested champion, an assassin of sentimentalism, a gaoler with a hardened heart. But I need to struggle against other people. This is what something deep down inside me commands me to do. There are times when I'm seized with a blind rage against other people as well as myself, I who live in a prison cell and don't know how to succeed in life.

If I were to run away I'd be so powerful... I can picture myself wandering round all alone, without fear of myself, without any cares, working and reading as much as I liked. And no one would recognize me, because I'd be living the life of a different person.

The last time I was tempted to run away, which unsettled me in a way it never had before, was after spending four hours talking to a vagrant who sat next to me on a bench on one of the main avenues. I was reading a novella by Panait Istrati. The man came and sat beside me, and asked if he could borrow my magazine. He read it quickly. Then we struck up a conversation. He was a young Jew, dressed in ragged clothes, and who had travelled and suffered a great deal. He told me about slaving away in the dockyards, and how it had crushed his shoulders. I realized that I would never be able to work as a docker, and this made me sad. He also told me about the strange existence of a pianist in suburban cabarets, who sails on Levantine steamers, disembarks in tropical ports, sleeps in squalid hotels and spends his nights playing in orchestras comprised of washed-up waifs and strays. My flesh quivered with excitement. It seemed that this was the only life that could bring me any peace.

The young man had fled from Bessarabia, and had been a waiter in a coffee house in Braşov, an apprentice in a tea salon in Constantinople, and then a nightwatchman at a timber yard in Smirna, from where he had stowed away again, this time on a Greek steamer to Cairo. He had stayed there for almost a year. He had never learnt English. He could read Russian, Romanian and French, and was intelligent but had had little education. He was afraid to tell me what his political convictions were, but I could guess.

We talked about Panait Istrati, who he adored. I tried to convince him that this parvenu writer from Braila didn't amount to much. With a smile the young man said that I was a 'bourgeois', and told me that I didn't yet understand Panait.

What didn't we talk about for four hours on a lonely bench in the noonday sun? And when we went our separate ways, I had quite different desires, walked differently, smiled differently.

When we met for a second time, it made me reflect on certain facts of life as it is really lived, which up till then I had only known about from hearsay and books. This thought process let me see things differently, gave me new eyes with which to view my companion less trustingly, and this escapade of mine with more caution.

We talked late into the night in an alehouse where he had insisted on going. I asked him how he had ended up in Bucharest. From what he told me, I got the impression that he was lying. He said that he had come from Hamburg, as a 'labourer', but didn't specify what his trade was. Carried away by his own words, he assured me that he had left Paris ten days earlier. He had forgotten about Hamburg. I could tell that he had spent a long time in France. He was too uneducated to remember so many names, so many places and so many extraordinary things simply from conversation or books. He spoke in a constant flow, warmly, sometimes using an *argot** that I couldn't always understand.

And then all of a sudden I started to disbelieve him. I saw him for who he really was, perhaps with suspicion in my eyes. I couldn't understand how he had managed to worm his way through so many countries as a labourer. I tried to catch him out. But my companion started to laugh, obviously delighted. Then he swore – a colourful expression, he assured me – in Russian. He told me that I was nothing but a 'bourgeois detective', and that I ought to work for the Sûreté, tracking suspects. Then he ordered a bottle of expensive wine, and began telling me all manner of things that interested me because of their originality, and the cynical way in which they were told.

In every town and city, the young man had lived on the earnings of a 'girl', always a different one. He had the strange ability to impose his will on street girls. He always chose the most beautiful ones. In this way he always had somewhere to live and money to spend. All day long he would roam around, smoking in the parks, and at night he played billiards in dingy cafés until it was time to meet his female companion.

As he told me all this he got more and more carried away, drinking one glass after another and trying to shock me with his immorality. I was disturbed not by what he said, but by the fact that I *approved of what he had done*. I searched within myself, and tried to find the merest feeling of revulsion, of disgust, and bit my lip in rage because his escapades aroused and seduced me.

It wasn't long before the idea of a life of hard work and vagrancy made me feel sad. I admitted my doubts to my new-found companion. He advised me to stay at home until I was mature enough to not be disgusted by a debauched and parasitic existence. Then he listed everything that I would need in order to run away. My birth certificate, my baccalaureate didn't matter, I would have to *steal* a lot of money from home, jewels, and to get a passport valid for a year, to become a Russian citizen at the legation in Constantinople, and get myself a job as a pianist on a third-class steamer that sailed between Alexandria and Nagasaki.

As I walked home I imagined myself at the height of a storm at sea, pounding the keys of a piano, my head spinning with the pitching and tossing, drunk from lack of sleep, fear and excitement.

When I got back it was late at night. Up in the attic, scents from the garden drifted in through the open windows. The wooden floor glowed in the moonlight. I fell into a happy sleep, determined to break with everything in my life that was mediocre, stifling and imposed by others.

I woke feeling dazed and disorientated after the wine I had drunk with my new companion, and from the dreams I had had. I realized that there were many things that still tied me to my home: the attic, my books, my novel. If I were going to leave, I would need money, courage, and the certainty that I wouldn't pine for my library. What prevents me from finding any peace is the fact that I yearn for books and the life of a vagabond at the same time and with the same consuming passion. I'm tortured by the desire to dedicate myself to austere, tireless and insane work, all the while equally tormented by the need to run away, to wander through a world of suffering. I have no idea how these yearnings will be resolved. Yet I believe that I lack the genuine willpower to choose certain aspirations, and to satisfy and achieve them...

*

It's even hotter now. And I haven't done any more work on my novel. Paper and notebooks await me in the drawer, but I read Anatole France and dream every night. I see my friends less and less. They've all gone their separate ways. It's for the best, I tell myself, without really believing that my happiness lies in solitude. I read constantly, from dawn till midnight, when I fall into a dazed and brutish sleep, my movements limp, like a man overcome by heat and lack of sleep.

I wait resignedly for the end of July, when I go camping in the forest of Sibiu. Scouting has always seemed an honourable yet dubious institution to me. We joined so we could travel by train for free. We have been on long excursions together, we've spent many wonderful nights in Dobrogea, we've wandered through the Bucegi and roamed the mountains of Neamt County. If I wrote it all down it would seem like literature. I find Boy Scout magazines and books suffocating. Their affected, unnatural style revolts me.

In the forest of Sibiu I'll pitch a tent for me alone, in the wildest, most isolated part. I'll spend my nights there, smoking and dreaming. Perhaps I'll write my novel. And perhaps I'll meet my heroine.

That part about the heroine is completely stupid. In the novel I'll write that I yearned for the forest, because in Bucharest the 'strong smells and passions' suffocate me. That has a lovely ring to it. One of our masters, a dark-haired, serious, scowling man who had a Prussian education, is always telling us this. If he were Headmaster, he says, he'd give us a military education. He refers to Bucharest as 'this inferno of seductions.' Which is strange: to me it's always seemed an inoffensive, dirty city. I like the forest, because I find it clean and enticing.

X

A Summer Diary

I'm back at home now.

I'm feeling rather tired and sad, as always after spending the night on a crowded train.

I didn't give my family many details. I just told that I came home early because I ran out of money.

Then I went up to the attic and slept till evening. I didn't dream of dark-haired girls, which made me unhappy while I was asleep but cheered me up when I woke. As I got dressed I whistled, and whispered to myself that I was very pleased with the way I had behaved. But as usual I was lying to myself, and with complete equanimity.

It was impossible for me to be pleased because I didn't understand a thing, *not a thing* that was going on deep down inside me.

The next day I read a lot. About two pages an hour. My eyes followed the letters but my mind was still in the forest of Sibiu. Or I stared at the poplar tree across the road and tried hard to feel sad. Despite the fact that no one was there to admire me, I did my best to strike 'interesting' poses. I knew perfectly well how ridiculous this was, but couldn't resist the temptation.

But the moment passed. This morning I woke up with a clear head, my mind sharp and exhilarated, my will unshakeable. Today I'm convinced that no one can stop me. I'm an unbeatable force. Once school starts again, my teachers are going to have to come to terms with this fact. Because I'm determined to put up with the boredom and overcome any obstacle that stands in my way; starting from this autumn I'm going to do some serious work – if only to test my willpower. I'll even revise so I get a brilliant mark in my retake, and humiliate Vanciu in the process. And I'll do it as soon as possible. So that people will finally know who I am.

It made me sad to read that last page. Three days have gone by, and I still haven't opened my maths books. This proves a great deal to me. It proves that...

But it's pointless trying to explain. I know that I simply don't have the willpower. I know that everything I write, I only write in order to stimulate this willpower that I don't posses.

But perhaps I just don't understand anything. Whenever I try to learn something about my inner life, I feel utterly bewildered. This autumn I'll have to study psychology in earnest. If only I knew more about myself then maybe things would be different. Yet it's so difficult to understand who I am. And I'm unable to analyse myself properly, because at the very moment when I need to look more deeply within me, my mind is suddenly filled with other things. Plus I don't know where to begin. It's easy to say: 'Above all know yourself!' But I'd like to meet someone who has managed to discover anything while trying to do this. I can't work it out. I can't distinguish between what exists naturally in my soul and what only exists in my imagination. I don't recognize myself in most of my thoughts, and can't fathom out the meaning of many of my emotions. I can't understand why sometimes I'm sad, and at others times I enjoy filling this notebook with common-place humour and trivia, when it should actually be overflowing with serious, in-depth analysis. But perhaps I'll find it easier to understand in the autumn, when I start studying psychology.

The other boys got back from camp today. They said they had a wonderful time. On the day before they left they took great delight in tearing down all the little buildings in the camp. I don't regret not being there.

Dinu told me in great detail about all his complicated love affairs. While he was in Sibiu he only fell in love with three girls, although seven fell in love with him. He told me their names, what they said, the songs they sang; using different facial expressions he acted out the girls' happiness, their suffering and despair; he read out passages from letters and showed me the originals.

Dinu is convinced that many girls will suffer because they yearn to be loved by him. He strolls down the street without a hat, and when he's sure no one is looking he arranges a kiss-curl over his forehead. He often comes to see me, and asks when I'm going to start working on my maths – so that he can start at the same time. I gave him my word – a grave and solemn promise – that on the twentieth of the month I would stop whatever I was reading and dedicate myself to maths. And that's what I'm going to do. I *must* do it. I know it'll be difficult, but if I put my mind to it I'll succeed. All I lack is the willpower.

20th August

Today I went to the school, where I read a half sheet of paper bearing an official seal and the Headmaster's signature, which announced that the retake examinations would begin on 15th September. This means there are twenty-five days of freedom left. Dinu and I agreed to put off revising for our exams until 1st September.

22nd August

Today I discovered Carlyle. In the notebook that I use for critical observation I wrote twenty-seven pages about him. I read *The Heroes* for the third time.

On 1st September I shall start revising maths.

29th August

I know the retake is getting closer and that I need to shut my books for two weeks. What complicates matters, however, is that Dinu brought me three volumes by Gourmont, one by Jack London, plus a collection of Samain's poetry. The books don't belong to him, and he asked me to finish them as soon as possible. It goes without saying that I can't miss the opportunity to read books that I've wanted to read for a long time. But when I finally do start revising maths, I'll only leave the house once every three days!

4th September

Haven't I always known? I'm far and away the laziest, most block-headed, incapable, lying coward in the whole of Greater Romania!

9th September

Only six days left. If I haven't learnt all the subject matter from start to finish by 15th September, then *I'll commit suicide*. It's the biggest decision I've ever taken in my whole life. I had to take it. Up till now, the heat in the attic and *Le Chariot d'or** have only allowed me to read thirty pages of algebra.

But now the decision is made. I've given my word of honour and I'll stick to that decision. If not...

What do I care about Christianity?

10th September

Three chapters of algebra, with explanations provided by Constantin Bărbulescu, a tall boy covered in red and white pustules and with a greasy nose – and who has moved up a year. It's a shame that the tram runs right past the house. It amuses me.

What's more, Bărbulescu explains things in a way that anyone could understand, speaking in a deep voice and waving a long pencil.

12th September

Dinu has been working with a private tutor for four hours a day (at a hundred lei an hour), plus four hours on his own. He's finished algebra and is halfway through trigonometry. In the evenings he strolls along the boulevard eating ice cream. He meets up with other friends who are retaking chemistry. They are all revising hard. Jipescu had read through his chemistry textbook three times by 15th July. Since then he has read his exercise book five times, his précis five times, a French treatise once, and his fifty-six pages of 'syntheses' eight times, which he hopes to be able to reproduce in the exam. Marcu is the only one who has been on the same chapter, 'chlorine', since August. If anyone asks him how he's going to manage, he says that he'll pass; if not, he'll repeat the year. In fact that's all that could happen to him. But the other boys say that Marcu is 'bluffing'.

13th September

It's impossible to know *everything* about maths. It would be better to revise a few chapters in depth, to understand them perfectly, and to just skim through the rest.

14th September

I've been giving it a lot of thought, and I think I'm right.

So what if I have to repeat my Lower Sixth year? Might this not be the very event, the spark that ignites the powder keg of my soul? Isn't this exactly what I need – a great calamity, a profound change that will set me on the right path in life?

I pictured myself downhearted, scorned by my friends, ridiculed by family and enemies alike, and I realized that only under these circumstances would I ever write *The Novel of the Short-Sighted Adolescent*, which would make me famous overnight, like Selma Lagerlöf, and rich, like Blasco Ibáñez[9].

So that's why I've decided not to revise for the retake. Vanciu, who has always disliked me, will just have to make me repeat the Lower Sixth year. That's precisely what I expect.

Perhaps I'll run away from home. How will I ever be able to write the novels that are in my mind if I don't know any real-life people in flesh and blood, especially a certain kind of person? I'll run away to the port of Constanța, where I'll take the advice of my vagrant friend from the summer, and become a *tapeur** on board a ship.

When I told Dinu about my decision he tried to make me change my mind, but his efforts were in vain. I know he's secretly delighted that he'll have a friend who leads a life of adventure, who writes successful novels, and who he'll be able to brag about in fashionable circles.

So just to poke fun at Vanciu and all the other mathematicians in the world, – an absurd and arrogant science – I'm going to spend all night reading *Les Messieurs Golovleff** by Shchedrin. It's a captivating novel that I bought from a second-hand bookshop the day before yesterday for only twenty-five lei.

15th September

The retake.

Emotions, heat, scornful words that that didn't ring true, suppressed shivering and a headache because I went to bed at two-thirty after finishing Shchedrin...

The written exam.

I couldn't remember anything. I didn't know anything. I tried to fill the pages with ridiculous calculations.

Dinu worked flat out. While, despite all their hard work, the others sat and stared at blank sheets of paper.

It was a very easy question, according to what I was told. From the nearby hall came the footsteps of friends, classmates, total strangers, all waiting for us to come out and tell them: 'How it went.'

To stop myself from shivering with fright, I thought of Blasco Ibañez.

And I stopped shivering.

I saw a dead leaf that had settled on the window sill. And I thought about how cold it would be in the port of Constanţa during the autumn. While up in my attic it's always warm in the autumn.

I handed in my sheet of calculations. Vanciu looked me straight in the eye.

Why didn't he smile?

At the blackboard.

However would I remember anything?

I gave a stupid answer. Or to be more precise, I didn't answer, I just resigned myself to taking the chalk from my classmate, walking up to the board and either pulling a face or standing there looking like an idiot, depending on my abilities and the circumstances.

Dinu 'muddled through' The others were like me. Whereas Mălureanu didn't even bother to pick up the chalk. What an honest boy.

Vanciu looked at us calmly, and wrote something on a piece of paper after each of our answers.

'Go and sit down!'

And that was the oral exam.

I'm at home now, writing in my notebook. Just so people know. I feel sleepy and very shaken.

18th September

Vanciu is a God!

He gave us a philosophical punishment: we all passed. A classmate who also had had to do the retake led us to understand that a female person had intervened on our behalf. But that doesn't make Vanciu any less deserving of worship.

One thing filled me with joy: I actually enjoy maths. It was only today that I realized this. It isn't difficult: on the contrary, there are many amusing aspects to it. Starting this autumn I shall take mathematics seriously. So that's settled. I've convinced myself that I have the willpower. An iron will, vast and infinite.

I also now realize that I didn't revise for the retake because *I didn't want to*. If I had *wanted* to, I would have read nothing but maths books for fifteen hours a day. What stopped me was the thought of running away from home. But now I've changed my mind, it's as simple as that. So I'll be able to study maths.

I'm going to relax for another two weeks and then I'll devote myself to maths. Maths and German.

Now I know who I am.

PART II

I

The Attic

In the distance, beyond the greyish-coloured houses, you can just make out two poplar trees. Two old, world-weary poplars standing in a courtyard surrounded by iron railings. When the poplars turn green I know it's springtime, and I say to myself: 'See, spring is here...' And I get up from my desk, open the window and look out at the street. Happy people are walking by and the sun smiles down at me. Whenever I look out of the window I'm faced with so many temptations... which is why I'm afraid to look out, so I settle down comfortably at my desk again.

My little room is gloomy in springtime. I don't mean it to be gloomy, that's just how it is. Outside there's plenty of sunshine and activity, and I can sense bees buzzing, trees blossoming, moist chestnuts glistening. The sun brings more light into my little room, but the light seems to pour out through the windows again. In here, everything is dead: the boxes of insects, the herbarium, the books on the shelves, the piles of magazines. A layer of dust lies over everything, and when evening comes it's quieter than ever.

It's then that my thoughts turn to the couples whispering to each other beneath the chestnut trees.

But in the cool, damp autumn I'm happy in my solitude. I stare at the embers in the brick stove and think: 'This autumn, perhaps I won't be alone when I stare at these embers, perhaps I won't be alone when I listen to the wind...' And then I laugh to myself: 'How many autumns have you spent wishing for these things?...' But it's as if I don't realize that when I bite my lip to stop myself from weeping, and wipe away my tears as I stare at the embers, I'm secretly indulging my deepest desires?

It was between these whitewashed walls, beneath this low ceiling, that my childhood came to an end. It is here that I was *'little'*. Where my red, wooden bed now stands there was once a cradle. I can remember so many moments, thoughts that I know will never return. 'My God,' I think, with a smile, 'I can't stay a child forever. I have to change, grow *big*, as big as I want to be. Or perhaps I'll have to suffer, be torn apart by sorrows, bedevilled by temptations. Is there really no other way?'

Why do I underline words in this notebook that no one will ever read? I'd love to capture the soul of this attic, the one I can feel, the one that reveals itself to me alone, in my solitude. So many years have gone by in silence, in gladness. I've had so many dreams in that red, wooden bed... I mustn't be sad if my dreams have remained dreams, if I haven't become a charmer, if I haven't travelled the length and breadth of India, if not a single Marie Bashkirtseff[10] has fallen in love with me... I now have new, sweet dreams. These dreams stretch all the way through my life, to me they seem like life itself, while to others they are only dreams.

Am I still unhappy? Perhaps no one will ever come up here to see me. Now, what shall I read?

My God! Books are so cold and foolish. There was a time when I used to glorify them in a thick notebook that I liked to call: *A Voyage around my Library*. At first I wanted to write a novel. I was the lover, fiancé and husband. My library was my beloved. But after a hundred pages, I realized that I would never write this 'novel.' Instead of describing a meeting between two lovers,

I extolled the virginity of books. I wrote commentaries on the women in Balzac's work, and convinced myself that there was more pleasure to be had from caressing an Elzevir[11] than a courtesan. I dedicated a whole chapter to books that contained signatures and dedications, another to the colour of covers, and another to publishers' insignia. Each of these chapters was six pages long. I had already written fifteen chapters. Then one evening it occurred to me that there was an absence of intrigue. This depressed me. So I abandoned the thick notebook with all its eulogies and dialogues. If I were to look for it in the chest now, I'd find it next to all my 'diaries', and accumulated writings. But I won't look for it now because I'm feeling happy, carefree and composed, and don't want to be overcome by sorrow.

What shall I write about, what should I write about to forget my sorrows? Perhaps this is the very reason that I'll write *The Novel of the Short-Sighted Adolescent*. But I don't have to think. I don't have to think, only write.

My attic looks out over a courtyard with a modest little garden. On the other side of the railings is the street. I don't know my neighbours. Why should I? None of them have a daughter. No, I can't put that in the novel. Instead I'll say that it's because I despise them.

When I'm sitting at my desk, through the little attic window I can see into the bedroom of the house next door. A happy young couple live there, who nobody knows. At lunchtime the husband brings home pastries. I usually return from school dejected, bashing my satchel against the fences and railings. Sometimes I see him hurrying home, red in the face, and then ringing the doorbell. I wonder: 'Will he kiss her?' And at those times I promise myself that I'll have a passionate little wife who'll kiss me and say my name in a clear voice, just like a laugh.

In the evening my wife lays out the tea things on a little, low table. I read in the shadows on the other side of the room so not to disturb them. I can't hear anything because of the noise of the tram. But they're speaking so quietly... this is what I tell myself, by way of consolation.

I read late into the night, when everything becomes still and is transformed, cold, mysterious, and blue. Suddenly the light goes out in my neighbour's bedroom. I smile over my book. She's kissing him now, I think, without a trace of anger. And I continue reading, my eyes growing tired. Then all of a sudden a light comes from the darkened bedroom again. I can't see very clearly, but I'm able to make out light bulbs shaded with cherry-coloured shawls, for a brief instant I see a lamp being put on a small bureau. And then once again, darkness. I hesitate: what am I to think? And I put down my book, which suddenly seems pointless and sterile.

But I start reading another book. Every so often I glance at my neighbour's window, where there is a faint light. 'For how many years have they loved each other?' I wonder, so as to not get angry. I promise myself that my wife will be blonde. And then I choose another book.

Later, after midnight, a light comes on in the window again. I smile: 'They're exhausting themselves, they're mad', I decide, piqued with envy and superiority. Naturally, the book I'm reading now seems dry. I go back to *Brand* or *Ecclesiastes*. I fall asleep thinking of the vanity of the flesh and the world. I fall asleep filled with a faint scorn for my neighbours.

But where did I get to? The soul of the attic, perhaps. How happy I am to be able to forget my sorrows. How happy I am to know that I'm going to write about the soul of my attic. How could I not know and love it when I've wept here so many times in the twilight, so close to it? It reveals itself to me alone. I find it in every book, in every painting, in every memory. The walls and bookshelves are infused with it. In winter, when I draw my armchair up to the stove, I see myself as I was many years ago, sitting next to this same brick stove on the Eve of St Vasile. Lying on my red, wooden bed, for the first time I give myself up to a sadness that my mother could never know. Only in autumn do I sit by the window. Working at my desk, I remember my very first, clandestine notebook, with these words written on the cover: *Novellas, vol. I.*

I live surrounded by all these translucent shadows, yet as I move forward they all remain in the same place, utterly alone, whenever the attic is lit up by the presence of my friends. At these times I notice them, and I alone smile at them. No one else has an inkling of the spell they cast. No one realizes that I would suffocate if I had to breathe any other air than the air in the little room where I learnt the letters of the alphabet using a sheet of cardboard. When I come in from the street, I caress the walls with my gaze. Their soul mingles with mine. What would happen if the attic belonged to someone else?

‖

'The Muse'

Cultural-Dramatic Society

'The Muse' holds meetings every Saturday, from four o'clock till eight. The current president of our Cultural-Dramatic Society is Miss Tanief-Alexandrescu. Miss Alexandrescu is one of our class-mates. She is in the Upper Sixth, but studies with a private tutor, so that she'll be able to start university next year.

Miss Alexandrescu is not a strict or inflexible president. Quite the opposite. She never arrives on time, never holds meetings, doesn't play the piano and won't act unless she can be Anca in Caragiale's *Năpasta*. It's the only role that suits her, she tells us. Nonetheless, our president is a very pleasant young lady, and no one would think of criticizing her for anything.

This autumn our Society has blossomed quite unexpectedly. 'The Muse' has won us over completely. Every week we get together and work enthusiastically: music, discussions, talks, recitals, plays. And at the end there is always tea.

The Society's headquarters are unique. One afternoon a week, our classmate Noschuna lets us use three rooms in the basement of his house. In fact it's thanks to these rooms that 'The Muse' came about. When we found out that we could have three rooms, we intellec-tuals and artists of the class set up the Society. This was last winter. We recruited members, elected a committee, – president, secretary, treasurer – chose an official letterhead, and established a monthly subscription. Last year it was five lei a month, this year it is ten.

We've had 'societies' all through our time at the lycée, but none of them have been as enjoyable as 'The Muse'.

In the Third Form we had to go to the meetings of the Fifth Form societies, where we learnt some very interesting things. The Headmaster gave lectures on morality; at the time, the Headmaster was an elderly man who was keen on morals. A member of the Sixth Form once spent an hour telling us about the evolution of matter, ether vibrations, the Einstein-Bergson debate and the value of syllogism in science. Another pupil read us a few of his short stories. There were some poets in the Fifth Form. They were quite prolific, because at every meeting they would take it in turn to read out dozens of stanzas. Those of us from the junior forms weren't allowed to leave, or to go to sleep, although they did at least allow us to not pay attention. And in any case, we were told that we wouldn't be tested on the content of the meetings.

In the Remove we formed a 'Study Group.' The first talk was given by Robert, who spoke about Racine. He had been inspired by Faguet. When he had finished, Leiber stood up and contested what he had said. According to him, Racine's inspiration was Brunetière. There was a heated argument. At the end of the evening, Robert walked out in high dudgeon, defying his opponent. At the second meeting there were five members. But the speaker didn't turn up. So we started playing games on the blackboard.

Yet 'The Muse' is completely different. To start with there are girls in 'The Muse'. Even some beautiful, jovial, daring girls. After every meeting we spend hours discussing the Society's activities and its delightful members – especially the delightful female members.

One of the first tasks of our Society was to print our own letterhead, and to buy make-up and wigs with the money we had collected from the members. After all, 'The Muse' is a dramatic society, and our hearts were set on acting. Nothing could stand in our way. Our recitations proved that most of the members were capable of playing a part on stage, and that all of us were eager to do so.

The rooms in the basement are ideally suited for performances. At the far end there is a drawing room with high windows that look out on the street. It is spacious and elegant, and also has a piano. Opposite the drawing room is a small room, which is longer than it is wide: *the stage*. The door between the drawing room and the stage acts as a discreet curtain. While they are getting ready for a play, the actors can wander around the stage dressed however they like, without fear of being seen. The prompter also opens and closes the curtain. He has to keep an eye on the drawing room door and ask: 'Who is it?' whenever he hears someone knock.

At the back of the stage there are two doors. One leads to the courtyard, the other into a small, dark room that was once used as a kitchen: the actors' dressing rooms. In this 'dressing room' our classmates transform themselves into the characters who appear on stage.

Last year we didn't manage to put on any public performances. We only did rehearsals. We tried playing some scenes from *Înşir-te Mărgărite* and *Năpasta*[12]. But this autumn, things have progressed. In less than two months we've successfully performed scenes from *Don Juan* by Victor Eftimiu and *The Devil's Disciple* by Molnár. There have been two lectures and quite a number of critical dissertations. And we've also played the piano in the drawing room.

We decided to perform *Don Juan* during the first week of term. We chose the final scenes. Don Juan was played by Robert – naturally. The Confessor, Father Ieronim, was me. Don Juan's page, Castagnete, was Dinu.

For Dinu and myself, 'The Muse' is providing our first experience of acting. Robert, on the other hand, has already performed in rehearsals of *Năpasta*. Het goes round telling people that he's an expert when it comes to the theatre. He never misses a play, cries during tragedies, buys a vast number of plays and knows numerous actors. He insists that he's an actor of the future, and declaims whenever he has the chance. So when he asked to play Don Juan, he wasn't turned down. It would be impossible to turn him down.

He told us that he had 'studied the role' and had 'drawn' a great deal from Victor Eftimiu's hero. So we were curious to hear him. The first rehearsal was at my house one evening, with Bricterian as prompter. Everything went marvellously. I was the only one who rushed and forgot his lines. But then I've never been able to remember long lines off by heart. If it weren't for the prompter I'd never dare appear on stage.

On Saturday we had our best meeting so far. We performed *Don Juan*, and all the actors were excellent.

A few weeks ago we started giving talks. I spoke about *Rama*, and Petrişor about Claude Farrère. My talk caused an uproar. It wasn't meant to last more than a quarter of an hour, but after a quarter of an hour I said that I had finished the introduction, and would now enter into the subject in detail. The committee protested, and after I had spoken for five minutes they stopped me. They said they would allow me to finish my talk on *Rama* at the next meeting. But I would still only get a quarter of an hour. My critics – Leiber the foremost among them – were delighted, and couldn't wait for the following week's meeting. They wanted to tear me apart in front of the other members. And there would be more members than ever on the Saturday that I was due to give my talk.

It was this that astounded me. I walked on stage with a serious expression, convinced that I was going to speak for a quarter of an hour, and that I would say everything I had to say about the Indian prophet. However, things went differently. A lot of girls had come. One of the members, Lia, had told the pupils in the Fifth Form that *I* would be speaking. As strange as it may seem, it was *me* who had attracted an enormous number of girls that particular Saturday. Lia had publicized me most enthusiastically as: 'An ugly and badly brought-up boy who doesn't speak French, doesn't understand English, doesn't kiss girls' hands and doesn't know how to drink tea, who reads a lot of philosophy, speaks quickly, waves his hands about and addresses girls with the familiar form of 'you', on top of which he blushes every five seconds and is extremely shy'.

According to her, I was a phenomenon. And Lia's classmates had fallen over themselves to come. What was all the more remarkable was that she had said that it was a talk about something they had never heard of.

Lia thought that I was going to speak *on stage*, just like I had spoken to her – a week earlier – and *sitting on a chair*. She thought I would bend over to tie my shoelaces, that I would forget why I had bent over and would play with them instead. She had thought

I would turn this way then that, gesticulating wildly, and pound my fists against the mirror...

I came onto the stage quite calmly. Once I got to the small table with a glass of water standing on it, I began: 'Gentlemen and ladies.'

Someone at the back corrected me: 'Wrong way round...'

I blushed. The girls – who were sitting in the first few rows – burst out laughing. They were all convinced that my talk was going to be hilarious.

'Gentlemen,' I repeated, 'Rama was the first Indian prophet. But this is of no importance.'

'Why's that?' enquired one of my many listeners, who was standing with his back against a wardrobe.

The girls thought this interruption was highly amusing, and that it was their duty to laugh. So laugh they did. It was a task that they performed easily and with great skill.

Not knowing quite how to react, since my audience were clearly filled with mirth, I picked up the glass of water and began to drink, although with little enthusiasm. For a moment or two the whole room appear to be moved that I should actually drink water from a glass. But it wasn't long before they exploded into roars of laughter again.

'Would you please not interrupt the speaker, I mumbled, putting the glass down.

The girls were quick to realize that this was a sign of great 'wit.' So they showed their appreciation by applauding.

At the back, meanwhile, the committee were getting agitated. There was a lack of seriousness. They hadn't expected this kind of scene, particularly not from me. Nonetheless they resigned themselves to having to wait until the end of the talk.

My talk continued in much the same atmosphere until I heard a voice from the audience: 'You have two minutes left.'

'But I haven't even finished the introduction.'

'Too bad.'

'It's not my fault. If I'm interrupted, I can't follow the train of what I'm saying. Why do you keep interrupting me?'

'It's not us who are interrupting you.'

'Then who is it?'

'Your girls...'

The word 'your' both disgusted and confused me. I searched for a 'forceful' response. Naturally, the girls started to laugh.

The committee asserted its authority: 'Sshh! Sshh!... Ssh!

'But it's already lasted fifteen minutes,' said one of the audience who were leaning against the wardrobe.

'Well? So what if it has?' snapped Lia, turning to look at him. 'Let him finish his talk. We're interested even if you're not.'

I – since I had convinced myself that they were genuinely 'interested' in the life of the prophet Rama – waited quietly for the audience and the committee to come to a decision. There was no more water in the glass.

The girls attempted to bring my talk to an entertaining conclusion. Because I hadn't yet finished speaking.

'Can you bring it to a close in five minutes?' said Noschuna, passing on the committee's ultimatum.

'The whole talk?'

'Yes, the whole thing.'

I smiled indulgently: 'It'll take a quarter of an hour just to finish the introduction.'

The girls knew they were supposed to laugh. So they laughed.

'Then we'll postpone it until next Saturday.'

'Fine. Next Saturday it is then.'

'What about the critical debate?' said Leiber, standing up, suddenly remembering that he was the Society's representative for the critical sciences.

'That will be next Saturday as well.'

Leiber thought for a moment, and then sat down again.

And yet this Saturday was our most successful meeting so far. Because the following week I didn't continue my talk. Petrişor's failed to arouse any enthusiasm from female members of the audience, and there was no 'performance' afterwards.

That evening, Mişu Tolihroniade suggested that we stage a few famous trials.

'What do you mean by famous trials?' asked a girl.

'In front of a jury chosen from among our members, we'll prosecute and defend some well-know personalities, such as Raskolnikov, for example.

The girls were very pleased at the idea of a trial involving Raskolnikov.

'But it will mean that between now and next Saturday, all members – male and female – will have to read *Crime and Punishment*.'

'*Crime and Punishment?*'

'Yes, the novel by Dostoyevsky.'

'But we haven't got it,' protested the girls.

'Then either buy a copy or we'll lend you one.' The girls' enthusiasm evaporated. Then Lia's face suddenly lit up.

'*Crime and Punishment?* Isn't it a thick, square book printed on poor-quality paper and with a yellow cover?'

'I don't know', said Mişu, apologetically. 'I read it in French.'

At this point I broke in, being an expert on the Romanian library.

'Yes, that's the one. It's published by Steinberg, with an introduction by Avramov.'

'Oh yes, Avramov... It costs forty lei...'

'No, thirty...'

'That's how much I paid... but that doesn't matter.'

We all waited impatiently to hear what Lia would say.

'It's a stupid, moronic book, it got on my nerves. That's what I think, and I've read it.'

'Did you read it to the end?'

'Do you think I'm an idiot or something? I read about fifteen pages and then threw it behind the bookshelf, from the sofa where I was sitting.'

'If you'd finished it you'd have a different opinion...'

'No, no, listen: it's stupid. Let's choose another trial.'

Mişu was against that idea. This was because a similar trial had been staged by a cultural society in Brăila, and he had been fortunate enough to hear to an outstanding summing up for the prosecution given by a student. Mişu had his heart set on putting Raskolnikov on trial so he could repeat the speech he had heard in Brăila.

But the committee postponed the decision for two weeks. They gave three members the task of choosing and presenting six characters from world literature that we could try.

We actors were the first to arrive. We found the owner of the house, Noschuna, stretched out on a sofa in the hall. He had violent stomach pains.

Despite being a doctor's son, he wasn't spared. His skin had turned a yellowish colour, and whenever he moved he walked doubled up. He asked us to forgive him, and to get on with the preparations and not worry about him. If we needed something we could ring the bell.

Faced with such kindness and self-sacrifice, we felt obliged to offer him some advice.

'Why haven't you taken smelling salts, old chap?' someone suggested.

'I can't take smelling salts.'

'Oh, but you should. You'll see how quickly you get better. In a trice.'

'I know... but I can't take... aah... ah... ah... agh!'

Then I said. 'Do you want us to rub you?'

'What do you mean, rub me?'

'We could rub your stomach. I've heard that it does a lot of good.'

Noschuna gave me an angry look.

'Give it a rest with this rubbing business, will you!'

'Go to bed then', we said, decisively. He didn't have anything to worry about. We'd handle everything.

So we set to work. First we had to get the scenery ready, before the audience – particularly the female variety – arrived. Because in order to get to their seats in the drawing room, they had to walk through the set...

I had brought two shrivelled rubber plants. The stage directions said: 'a garden in Don Juan's palace.' Two rubber plants didn't make a garden; we obviously realized that. But it was a start.

High up on the wall at the back of the stage there was a small window. We covered it with a tablecloth. We had also brought a blue abat-jour*[13], which we put over the light bulb, because the scenes take place at night.

Next we started preparing the actors' costumes. Robert, Don Juan, had had a black velvet waistcoat made. He had also found a peculiar pair of trousers, which, he claimed, gave him a 'period' appearance. He would also wear a blue beret, like those that were fashionable among young men during the Renaissance.

His was a school beret, however, like the girls wear, and only very slightly modified.

The costume worn by Dinu, who was playing *Castagnete*, Don Juan's page, was delightful. This upset Robert, because he didn't see why a servant's costume should be more elegant and costly than that of his master, Don Juan. Dinu's explanation was very simple: he didn't have anything else, and didn't want to wear anything else.

So he had brought it with him. It consisted of short, puffed trousers, long black stockings, and a *phantaisie** style tunic made of yellow silk with black stripes. The collar and cuffs were white lace. He also had a black, curly wig, something else that Don Juan didn't have. And so Don Juan was upset – most of all because he had a crew cut, like all the other boys at the Spiru Haret Lycée. All he could count on were his talent and good looks.

My costume was the simplest of all. I was playing the priest, Father Ieronim, Don Juan's confessor. I had borrowed my father's long black coat, which came down to my ankles. Instead of a clerical skull cap, I wore the end of a stocking on my head.

I also needed to whiten my hair. I went and asked our benefactor: 'Noschuna, can you let me have some talcum powder?'

'Of course, but what do you need it for?'

'You know I'm playing Ieronim, and I have to have white hair.'

'You're right. But wouldn't it be better if you used flour?'

'Flour?'

'Yes, because you'd need too much talcum powder. Shall I ring for some?'

'Okay.'

The maid brought a yellow metal container, and said I could have as much flour as I wanted. Using a small spoon I poured flour onto my head, and then rubbed it so it went right down to the roots. I was worried that it might not come out a definite colour. It wasn't exactly pleasant; flour got into my ears and went down my collar. Whenever I moved my head even slightly, it sprinkled over my eyes and eyebrows and turned them white. So I had to keep my neck still.

By now, Don Juan and Castagnete had started putting on their make-up. The page was quite an expert. He had fixed on his wig, powdered his face, rouged his lips and cheeks, and darkened his eyelids with a black crayon. From a short distance he looked like an Adonis. Don Juan, however, had no idea how to use make-up. He had powdered his hair at the temples, but not properly. He had tried to trace two lines across his forehead, but they were so wide that he had to wipe them off with a wet handkerchief. Around his eyes he had drawn dark rings that looked frightful. Then he just put some rouge on his lips.

'Don Juan is pale,' he assured us.

By now we had moved into the actors' dressing room, because the audience had started to arrive. The dressing room was in complete uproar. Water had been spilt on the tables, and an unbound copy of *Don Juan* was disintegrating beside a glass pitcher. In the corners there were piles of shoes and stockings, trousers hanging on nails, the make-up case, a bottle of eau de cologne, a cloak and two rapiers. Our benefactor was totally unaware of all this. He was in the hall, looking after the female members of the audience. Nearly everyone from our Society was there, along with a few guests from St Sava Lycée. Through the wall we could hear Petrişor's laugh as he flirted with Lia. No doubt he was sitting near her and telling her that she had delightful calves.

Ten to four. We were due to start at four. The only people missing were Miss Tanief-Alexandrescu and Leiber. Come what may, we had to wait for our president.

We actors were impatient and emotional. We paced up and down, rehearsing our lines in our heads, glancing through our parts and looking in the mirror. Robert insisted that he wasn't nervous; that he was used to being on stage; and that he enjoyed performing in front of crowds and winning them over.

It was now dark in the hall; on stage, we lit the lamp with the blue *abat-jour*. Bricterian, who prompted from behind a large trunk, slowly opened the door. My heart was pounding as if it would burst. I hardly dared steal a glance into the hall. As if through a mist I could make out all the pairs of eyes, feasting on the light, the rubber plants and the cast.

I began with a great outburst. I was a Father Confessor, my name was Ieronim and I wanted to take all of Don Juan's possessions for my monastery. I gave an enthusiastic performance, and kept my gestures to a minimum. Although I'd kept my glasses on, I was still afraid that I'd get flour in my eyes. I acted in a way that I knew was 'good.' At the last rehearsal I had been told that I was 'unrivalled' when it came to playing Ieronim.

What was more, Bricterian prompted with great skill from behind the trunk – although occasionally he whispered too loudly and could be heard in the hall. So while Don Juan was making his first reply, I took the opportunity to gesture to him that he was too loud.

After a few minutes, my fears evaporated. I walked calmly on stage and confronted Don Juan. Leaning against the dressing room door, which was out of sight of the audience, Dinu looked on and encouraged us.

Whenever Don Juan had to say more than half a dozen lines, I studied the audience and tried to gauge their reaction. They were very impressed.

As I had expected, I got muddled a few times, and Don Juan missed a few of his lines. But the audience didn't notice at all.

Then Castagnete came on. Dinu had never claimed that he had any dramatic talent. Yet he was wearing a divine costume, and the female members of the audience couldn't take their eyes off his fake curls. Don Juan became more passionate. He pounded his fists, clenched his teeth and glowered. But the girls didn't look at him.

Every scene was a triumph. When the play ended, the house lights went up. We were applauded and had to do two 'curtain calls'. We were in seventh heaven. But then Don Juan and I felt terribly depressed. Because we now had to take off our costumes and go into the hall dressed like everyone else. Dinu, on the other hand, had actually come in his page costume. He strutted about, garnering the admiring looks of all the females. Each of them made a complimentary remark and smiled sweetly at him.

'Oh, you were so good!... Wonderful'.

'Do you think so, gracious lady?'

'Very, very good indeed!'

Dinu gave a modest laugh: 'Ha, ha, ha, ha!'

The two Dinescu girls were also there, short, plump, without a trace of powder on their cheeks and wearing dresses buttoned to the neck. The older one secretly pined for Dinu. Her younger sister 'had a liking' for Fănică. She sat next to him while we had tea, served him and laughed flatteringly at his jokes. Fănică is resigned about it. Miss Dinescu completely lacks charm. She barely says a word, because she's shy. She doesn't approve of 'modern' jokes and always walks in a very staid, upright manner.

As usual, Lia and Irina were sitting on the sofa next to the stove. They were wearing short dresses that came to the knee, and seemed pleased whenever they noticed someone's gaze caressing their legs. Petrişor and Dinu were sitting beside them. In the second row, four other girls were chatting to Bricterian and Morariu. At the back, next to the bookcase, the committee were discussing Dinu's behaviour. Robert was disgusted. He said it was 'immoral', that it was annoying members of the Society. Leiber accused Petrişor of being frivolous and 'flirtatious.' Mariana Tanief-Alexandrescu wasn't happy with the 'bevaviour and attitudes' of Misses Lia and Irina. I listed to the discussion with interest. It was decided that they would be given a warning.

Tea. The usual tea party, where you have to smile, laugh at the host's jokes and serve the people sitting next to you, who always say: '*Merci*, you're too kind!'

Dinu got up and headed towards the dressing room. He said he had to change out of his costume. Miss Sasa – dark skinned, with wild hair like Salomé, full lips and large eyes – followed him. There was an awkward silence. We all sipped tea from our porcelain cups. A few people tried to make jokes, but they fell flat. Even Petrişor said nothing. The Misses Dinescu blushed, and Mariana was lost in thought. Questioning glances were directed at the door.

It went on like this for about a quarter of an hour. We were about to get up and thank our host when the pair reappeared, flushed and shameless.

Once the other members had left, the committee got together. The next morning at school, I heard that Dinu, Petrişor, Sasa, Lia, and Irina had been excluded from the Cultural-Dramatic society 'The Muse'.

Dinu laughed, and announced that he would organize a far more exciting society than 'The Muse', at his house.

Nonetheless, Robert had still won.

Fănică

Fănică has written a 'variety show'. He calls it *A Model Lycée*, and plans to stage it on St Spiridon's Day. There is always a festival for St Spiridon. It begins with an address, followed by performances from the band and the choir, poetry recitals, and finally games and gymnastics. St Spiridon is a day to remember. All week long the Headmaster smiles benevolently at everyone, doesn't set tests, doesn't take in our German vocabulary lists or give much homework. Not only that, the masters all arrive late for class.

This year, however, the festival will be unique, because we'll be performing *A Model Lycée*. And it's about our lycée. The characters are our masters, and Fănică has shared out the parts among us. The 'Headmaster' will be played by Bricterian. This is because Bricterian is the best actor among us. He's tall, walks on stage with great aplomb and accentuates every word. Ever since the Fourth Form he's been in every school play on St Spiridon's Day, and he's also acted for 'The Muse'.

Fănică himself will play two parts. The first is a father angry about tuition fees, and the second, a pupil who caught jaundice in the chemistry class. No one else was suited to the role. All this spring, Fănică has been nursing a grudge against Toivinovici. Toivinovici hasn't actually picked on him, but Fănică is faint-hearted by nature, and has an extraordinary horror of chemistry. This spring – terrified by the formulae of organic acids and acyclic series – he became ill, contracted jaundice, and was bed-ridden until the end of April. It was during this time that he decided to write the 'variety show'.

Act I takes place in the staff common room, and is a dialogue between a pupil suffering from jaundice and a chemistry master. It is written in rhyming couplets and is extremely witty.

I play the part of Toivinovici, probably because I have red hair and know the formulae for acyclic series. When Fănică first gave me the news, I laughed nervously and clapped him on the shoulder. Fănică smiled sweetly, like a real theatre director, and said I'd be a great success. Our scene is one of the best, because Fănică put a great deal of passion into writing it, remembering the weeks he'd spent in bed with jaundice. And he'll play the part with just as much enthusiasm.

All the other boys are convinced that I'll play the part of the 'red dog' perfectly. They reminded me of the part I played for St Spiridon last year, an assistant police commissioner. I sat at a desk facing the audience, and tried to get their attention with a 'comedy sketch' that I'd just made up. For instance, I pretended I couldn't write because my pen had broken. In my view, this would give rise to a whole series of hilarious gestures and expressions.

As it turned out, the sketch was quite a success. At one point I had to bring the chief commissioner a cup of coffee from backstage. As I came through the door, someone handed me a tray and suggested I walk slowly, so as not to spill the cup of coffee or the glass of water. This piece of advice terrified me. At the director's request I had taken off my glasses. So when I came back with the chief commissioner's coffee, I tried to walk as carefully as possible. I appeared on stage with my head bowed, arms trembling and legs like jelly. Everyone thought that it was my own 'creation' and enjoyed it enormously.

I had also acted in plays put on by 'The Muse'. But very few of the other boys had seen me.

Fănică described the other scenes to us. In Act I, Scene I, four man-about-town type boys are dancing in the Headmaster's study. They have come to complain to the Headmaster that their teachers won't allow them into the classroom. They won't let them in because their hair is too long. The man-about-town boys are outraged. If they have to have their hair cut once more, or if they have to put 'numbers' on their tunics, they won't dare attend another tea party or ball. But as the Headmaster isn't in his study, the man-about-town boys dance. Then they each sing a verse about the 'tea rooms', *Petit Parisien** and *La Garçonne*.*[14]

While Fănică hummed the verses in a squeaky voice (he's not a tenor), the others speculated about who would play the parts of the man-about-town boys. They would have to be good-looking, have fashionable tunics and know how to sing and dance. Robert was sure to be one of them. When he heard this, he half-closed his eyes and accepted. Modestly, he told us that he would be 'best for the part'. The second man-about-town boy would be Gianii. Gianii has never acted, either at school or in 'The Muse'. He doesn't know how to recite lines and can't sing. But Gianni is a genuine man-about-town boy. He uses talcum powder, wears cologne, speaks French, is quite chubby and loves dancing. When the playwright offered him the role, Gianni blushed. He was embarrassed, and looked at us all with great affection. In turn we all smiled sweetly at him, and gave him encouraging looks.

The third man-about-town boy is Locusteanu. He elbowed the playwright in sheer delight, and cried out inanely: 'Hey golly Fănică!' Fănică smiled at him and suggested that he eat raw eggs before the performance, to improve his voice. There was then a discussion about who should be the fourth man-about-town boy. Moraniu didn't want the part. He said he didn't know how to sing. And yet Morariu has a tunic that is far too elegant to not be in the scene. Fănică wouldn't give up. He promised him that he could sing as quietly as he liked. He might even be able to speak his verse, because the orchestra would play the melody. Still Morariu refused. But some people were sure that he would accept eventually.

Dinu was with us and seemed very taken with the idea of the 'variety show'. I think he'd be delighted to play the part of one of the man-about-town boys. He hasn't forgotten his success with 'The Muse', when he appeared as Don Juan's page, with his black wig and yellow silk cape. But he isn't at our lycée any more. More than anything he wanted to have long hair this year, so he moved to the Matei Basarab Lycée, where they don't have to wear uniforms or caps.

Fănică began to sing the verse sung by the father angry about tuition fees. The boys listened enraptured, and smiled whenever he looked at them. Every time he paused they applauded wildly.

Some of them asked him to explain the script, which Fănică was delighted to do.

Fănică is short and skinny. After humming so many verses written for a tenor he was completely out of breath, and had to wipe his forehead with a handkerchief. He was exhausted. But when he got to the scene where a pupil who has just taken the Baccalaureate celebrates the joys of liberty and long hair, he sang with renewed energy. He closed his eyes and set his jaw, because this part was also for a tenor. He went red in the face and his eyes filled with tears. But it was a total success. Robert – who knew he was going to play the part of the pupil – laughed heartily and congratulated the author. The pupil's costume was discussed. Robert thought he should wear modern clothes, patent leather shoes and a silk scarf. But Fănică disagreed. The boy was coming to the Headmaster's study to collect his Baccalaureate certificate. So he could only be wearing school uniform with a number on his tunic.

Robert was disappointed, but accepted the decision. I know he very much wanted to appear on stage wearing fashionable clothes and make-up so as to impress the girls in the audience. Nonetheless, he was sure that he would carry the day. He boasted that he would be applauded from Act I Scene I onwards. And then he gave Dinu a knowing look. Dinu was smoking.

When he got to Act II, Fănică speeded up the pace. As the curtain rose, the orchestra would play a triumphal march.

The masters had come to the Headmaster's study to protest about the 'Lalescu Scale'.[15] They were dissatisfied with their salaries, and each one came forward in turn to sing his own praises. Here, Fănică showed himself to be quite malicious. By extolling the masters, he drew attention to their weaknesses. The boys all applauded enthusiastically.

*

We were approaching the Călugărească Valley, and were impatient to see Morariu's vineyard. He had invited us spend that Sunday at his family home. He told us there would be young girls who had come to work on the grape harvest, as well as plenty of *must*[16].

There would be old wine too. But no one seemed particularly interested in Morariu's wine, new or old.

During the day we ate grapes and threw clods of dirt at each other in the vineyard. We split into two groups: cops and robbers. The cops had to catch the robbers. Fănică laid down the rules: we weren't allowed to throw large clods, or to aim for people's heads. Plus we had to own up when we were hit. And when a robber was hit he had to stay where he was.

I was a robber, and put up a heroic defence against Petrişor and Manu, using an acacia branch. But in the end I had to run for it. I tripped over a pile of wooden stakes, and the police threw clods at me but missed.

Later on I freed two of my fellow robbers, and I hit Robert in the back with a clod of dirt as he was bending down to tie his bootlaces.

In the evening there was a big meal. But I fell asleep quite early, because I'd been made to drink numerous glasses of red and white wine. The others stayed up till dawn. There was no shortage of girls, but the boys took little notice of them, because Morariu's father was never far away.

IV

The Editor

Determined to get the money that I was owed by the literary review run by Mr Leontescu, on the pretext of having 'family matters' to attend to I was allowed to miss the third period, which was gym. I rushed home and took off my tunic and cap. Mr. Leontescu thinks I'm a student. It is on this that I pin my hopes. The editor of this literary feuilleton – as well as the newspaper that publishes it – is very kindly disposed towards students. We've spent long hours together, bewailing the woes of university life. As far as Leontescu knows, I'm studying literature, which is why he bores me with advice about my future career as a journalist. Sometimes he says I'm sure to follow in his footsteps.

As I walked up the mirror-lined staircase I felt rather nervous. Yet it wasn't timidity or fear. I was accustomed to knocking on publishers' doors, walking hesitantly towards a man behind a desk and asking in a hushed voice if I could speak to the editor-in-chief. And I've had some modest success. One evening, on hearing my name, a man gave me a friendly smile and shook my hand warmly. I was so touched that I didn't have the courage to ask if I'd be paid for my articles. I asked him a week later, however, and was greeted with the same warm handshake.

On another occasion, the editor praised an article of mine that he had published on the front page. I smiled proudly for the entire time he was talking to me. But even then I didn't get a penny. He told me that the magazine's sales were down, that money was tight, and that he himself was barely able to live on what the director paid him. Yet this editor was elegantly dressed and was always buying French books.

I first met Mr Leontescu last summer. He published everything I sent him in large white envelopes. Occasionally I wrote to him, telling him about my difficult life and leading him to believe that I was a penniless student who he might be in a position to help. I tried to sound despondent. I put all my efforts into writing doleful letters, which I signed with my full name and address. And then, filled with trepidation, I would wait for a whole week. The editor published all my articles, one after another. And yet no reply arrived, either at my house or via the publisher's internal mail.

At one point I went into detail: for the twenty articles that he had published so far, I asked five hundred lei – ie: twenty-five lei per article. It wasn't much. Plus I offered him other articles I was working on, for the same price. Not only that, I offered him numerous pages of comments for free.

As usual, several weeks passed. The fact that I could remain so calm began to torment me. So I decided to pay the editor a personal visit.

I finally got to meet him this summer. I came across him in the editorial office, smoking idly among piles of newspapers. He had a narrow, furrowed brow, and shrewd eyes behind a pair of thick-lensed glasses. He greeted me enthusiastically. He didn't offer me a seat, but praised my articles about Romani Rolland. In my opinion these were my worst. He said he liked my 'broad horizons' and 'the way I expressed myself'. He spoke in short bursts, blinking continually. He told me that my contribution had become indispensable to the review. Then he introduced me to a gentleman who had come in later, and who shook my hand somewhat distantly, without getting up from his chair.

But I failed to mention anything about payment. Nonetheless, the editor asked me to drop in and see him whenever I had a moment. I promised I would. And naturally I also promised him more articles.

A few weeks later I paid him another visit. His glasses were lying on the desk, and he was scratching his head. He gave me a withering look; I had disturbed him. So yet again I didn't dare ask about payment. When I left he shook my hand and wished me luck with my work. And I promised him more articles.

But I didn't lose heart. I knocked on the door of the editorial office one Friday evening, when I knew he would be alone. He was correcting the leading article: 'Delighted! Delighted!' I waited until he had finished. Then he looked at me in a kindly way, and asked how I was getting on with my study of the Orient. Enthusiastically I told him about my reading and my plans. The editor seemed interested. He smiled. So I came straight to the point, with a calmness that took me by surprise. The editor hesitated, and wiped his glasses with his handkerchief. I looked him in the eye, and could feel my cheeks blazing. Then he broke the silence in the most pusillanimous way. He promised that he would speak to the director. He said that my articles were really 'good', that he liked my 'broad horizons' etc etc. That he would keep reminding the director. That he understood my situation. But what else could he do? The director made all the decisions, he himself was of no importance. Then we shook hands rather half-heartedly.

I haven't seen him since.

*

But then today, during the gym period, I walked up the mirror-lined stairs once again. I'm a well-known figure in the corridor that leads to the editorial office. The doorman knows me, as do the doorman's two assistants, and the attendant who sits on a bench against a wall and asks whoever walks in: 'How may I help you, sir?'

Today, however, he wouldn't let me into the editorial office.

'May I ask your name, sir?'

I told him in a dignified, sonorous tone. He went into the editorial office. I could just make out a few words, and recognized Mr Leontescu's voice. I prepared my opening remarks: I was sure he would see me immediately.

'Mr Leontescu asks if you wouldn't mind waiting for a few minutes.'

I sat on the bench. I tried to look blasé. In fact I could barely control my feelings of disappointment. The attendant sat next to me, quite calmly. And I began to plot a terrible and exquisite final revenge.

I imagined myself as a famous young man, the author of numerous published works, his picture in all the leading literary reviews. I would walk right past Ilie Leontescu in the street. Just as I was about to quench my thirst for vengeance, my thoughts were interrupted by a stupid question from the attendant. I remembered I was here to visit the editor and frowned. I tried to calm myself. The editor was probably writing an article that couldn't be delayed. Or he had to check the final proofs. Silently I counted to fifty. I stopped. I would count to twenty, and then I would knock on the door.

'Nineteen...' between nineteen and twenty there was a long pause. I stood up.

'Twenty.' I walked in. The editor was gazing absent-mindedly out of the window. The room was hot, and he was in his shirt sleeves. At another desk, a man who looked half-asleep was listlessly translating something from a book with yellow covers. 'Good morning', I said loudly.

Curious, the editor stared at me. Then he recognized me and held out his hand. He asked me to sit down, something he had never done before.

'Please, have a seat.'

'Thank you.'

Subdued, I walked over to him. In his shirtsleeves he looked like an inoffensive sort of man.

'What did the director say, Mr Leontescu?'

'The director?'

He have me a puzzled look from behind his glasses.

'What was the director supposed to say?'

'You know... You promised.'

It was only then that the editor realized who I was. He frowned, and ran his hand over his forehead. Again he asked me to sit down, and looked at me sadly. I understood. I decided to have it out with him once and for all.

'I did speak to him. Everything will be fine. I assure you it'll be fine. I explained to the director that...'

The expression on my face rather undermined him.

'He said it'll be fine, but that you'll have to wait till Christmas. That's when the editorial budget increases. And you'll be the first to be paid.'

He rambled on, clearly embarrassed. I smiled. Then suddenly he looked up and stared at me from behind his glasses.

'Are you short of funds?'

I was tempted to exaggerate: 'I'm completely broke.'

The editor looked at me sympathetically: 'It'll be fine... you have my word.'

I was tired and thoroughly fed up. I had humiliated myself and had nothing to show for it. The editor had won. The editor always wins.

He showed me the corrections for my latest article. And I got a brief glimpse of the front page of the review. I blushed.

'What else are you working on?'

Smiles.

'You have plenty of talent...'

Smiles.

'I'll publish anything you write. I have confidence in you.'

Smiles.

'What do you say, young man?'

'What can I say, sir?'

'Life is what you make of it!'

'Precisely...'

'Just never lose heart.'

'...'

'You have no right to. You're young.'

'...'

'If I told you everything that I've been through, eh!'

'I can believe that, sir.'

'So much, young man, so much...'

'...'

'I'll have you know that I've written a whole collection of poetry that I still haven't found a publisher for...'

'...'

'A publisher, sir, do you hear me? It's unbelievable.'

The editor was getting carried away. Every now and then he scratched his head. I smiled at him. He talked to me for quite a long time. Then eventually we shook hands and bowed to each other.

I realized that victory belonged to the editor.

I went back to school, dejected.

Fourth period had already started. But I made a solemn promise to myself that day, never to send anything else to Mr Ilie Leontescu. Even though I have plenty of talent. Even if he does have confidence in me, and even if I could actually write...

November

So now I know. I'm just like all the rest: a dreamy, sentimental adolescent. There's no point trying to hide it. I'm sentimental. I'm ridiculous.

On this November afternoon I'm feeling sad. Although there's no reason for me to be sad. I don't have to be sad... I'm looking out of the window at the poplars. And I'm lost in thought. Naïve thoughts, idiotic and sickeningly naïve. How hard I've tried to uproot this weakness from my soul, a weakness that goes by the name of melancholy.

I'm melancholic. Therefore I'm stupid. I lack motivation, virility, personality. Why should I be melancholic this afternoon, when the sun is shining through the leafless trees? Why am I looking out of the window instead of getting on with my work? Why do I dream of being a rich and handsome man strolling through empty parks, with their moss-clad fountains, statues bathed in the blood-red rays of the setting sun, and ivy covering the bridges and castle walls?

Times like these only bear witness to my lack of willpower. Instead of fighting against the foolish nostalgia of the November sunshine by whipping myself until I bleed, I sit writing in a notebook that no one will ever read.

So many efforts have been in vain this afternoon... so many hours spent with my teeth clenched, so many hot, moonlit nights enticing me to dream and roam the streets, nights spent all alone and which came to nothing. But all my tears, my pride, the sufferings of my flagellated body are powerless when confronted by a November day.

It was bound to happen. In fact I've been waiting for this day, when I would stop work and just stare out of the window. Week by week my willpower has slowly evaporated. And now today, disaster has struck. Instead of thrashing myself, resisting myself to my last breath, I sit here calmly writing. Perhaps I think this is a way of paying off my debts.

A November day. A day like any other. The sun is sad, and from all sides come strange stirrings. A warm day. A day when old men and women think about the past and weep. But what do I have to be sad about? Why do I feel as if my soul is filled with unfamiliar, sweet, terrifying sensations? Why do I want to cry? Why am I waiting for something that I know will never come?

But I'm not going to indulge myself with any of this. I'm not like other adolescents, a naïve dreamer, sickly, foolish, sentimental and ridiculous. My soul is made of sterner stuff. My will might be absurd, yet it is still firm, formidable, thrusting aside and choking off all that stands in its path. I have to be the same person at all times and in all places. Solid as a rock, brows lowered, eyes fixed on my goal, lips clamped firmly together in rage, fists clenched ready to strike myself, to inflict pain on my flesh. That is how I should be. Because that is what I want to be. Me, the one and only master of my body and soul, the only male in the flock of spineless adolescents, the only one with the willpower to grip an iron bar in my teeth until they shatter, to whip myself until I scream, until my flesh is burning, as agonizing as an open wound.

That is how I should be. Like I used to be in the days when I took pleasure in inflicting pain on myself. The days when I woke at dawn and went to bed after midnight. When I drove away sleep with my fists. When I read till my eyes filled with tears and my eyelids stung. Until my head grew heavy and my eyes grew dim. Until my mind clouded over.

The days when I used to whip myself.

Those were the most wonderful days of my life. I kept my whip behind a bookshelf. Every night before turning out the light, I would indulge in fifteen minutes of sweet, painful pleasure. I gripped the rope, doubled it over and counted to ten. The first blow – thrown over my shoulder with my eyes closed – bit into my bare, white, fleshy back. I stifled a scream. This was the most agonizing blow of all. After that the rope fell faster and faster, cut deeper and deeper.

My flesh quivered, my cheeks trembled, my lips drained of colour. I kept my eyes tightly closed so I wouldn't see the rope falling. The pain excited me. I lashed ever faster in short, sharp strokes. My flesh began to swell, to catch light. My temples were ablaze, salty sweat trickled down my forehead. But I savoured this triumph of the spirit. The will that trampled my putrid flesh filled me with an enthusiasm that was both holy and virile. As my flesh moaned, I whistled victoriously through clenched teeth. Pain and pleasure mingled in a frenzy I had never known, and I drank it down in a delight that was beyond price. It was the only pleasure I allowed myself.

After this came a moment of ecstasy. The pain brought me closer to myself; purified me. That one moment was my reward for an entire day's work. A single moment. Followed by exhaustion, inner turmoil, trembling. My body felt utterly spent, as if after an illness. I barely had the strength to put the rope back behind the bookshelf, and to cover my scourged back with my shirt. Warm blood would sometimes trickle down from my shoulders to my waist. The blood stained my shirt, and I had to get up at dawn to wash it.

But there were times when pleasure and pain didn't overwhelm me. I would often pace up and down impetuously, but my limbs wouldn't tremble when my shirt touched my shoulders, which were striped by the whip.

There were victorious days when I shouted the word 'I' at the top of my voice. When I was intoxicated with myself. When I was dazed by the vortex that I could feel ravaging my soul.

With my eyes closed like a visionary, I would shout: 'I, I, *I*, *I*...' And I look back on those days with sorrow, now I'm sad that the sun is shining through the leafless trees.

I wish I had a soul like Brand's. A tortured soul, harsh and solemn. Yet beneath which was concealed the white-hot lava of enthusiasm, love and hate. I knew it wouldn't be long before my voice would be feared and envied throughout the land.

Yet I didn't want – and still don't, even now – to expose any of my anxieties, or the dark shadows and flames of my soul.

No one should see me exhausted from the fight; nor should anyone know the name of the God for whom I struggle.

I wanted to be able to move among my fellow men unrecognized. To be regarded as an ugly, boring adolescent, while all the time my mind and soul were made of rock. To suddenly appear, to subdue the cringing herd and reduce those who despised me to impotent astonishment. To whip them, to desecrate their faces, to glory in the sensation of my body quivering with fruitfulness and creativity.

I have never enjoyed having friends. I had no desire to bare my soul to some pallid, melancholic adolescent. The pride of knowing that I had a secret that no one would ever guess was enough for me.

The thought that one day I would terrify whole multitudes of human beings intoxicated me. I knew who I was. This filled my soul with boundless confidence, forcing me to flex the muscles in my arms as if in preparation for the fight. And most of all, because *no one* had any idea who I was, who I would become.

But that's not how things really were. Like all weak people I have sought friends. In myself I recognized a soul in search of consolation and support. I've uncovered certain dark corners of my secret, and let other people see things that, by rights, only I should know. I wanted to be merciless. But I've never succeeded. I've been fickle and quick to compromise, like any adolescent. I've told jokes, I've laughed more than necessary, I've wasted time talking to stupid classmates and boring friends, I've slept for eight hours solid like all the others, and at night I've wandered the streets, baring my soul; I've stolen glimpses at women with warm bodies, and lost my innocence one rainy night in a damp little room, on a bed where dozens of other bodies had once entwined, accompanied by the laughter of those waiting outside the door.

I, just like all the rest. I, just like the herd. Just like any other spineless, lecherous adolescent, who sleeps for fifteen hours on Sunday, laughs loudly, flirts with young ladies at tea parties, pinches women who walk past him in the street at night, dances in night clubs, bets on the horses, reads *Rampa*, loves Mosjoukine[17] and tries hard to be blasé. Like Robert, who admires Musset...

And that's not all. I've disregarded the best decision that I ever made: to preserve within me, in order to perfect them, all those things that I intended to bestow on others at a later date.

But instead of striding out with a proud, sure tread, with my ideas still intact and my books completed, I've revealed myself little by little in the form of articles in popular magazines, on pages where my heart and soul are not to be found, in lines devoid of éclat or originality.

With difficulty – like all the others – I've gained a place for myself in second-rate literary reviews, who published my articles with spelling mistakes and without my full name.

There is so much baseness fermenting in my soul, that I've waited impatiently for a translation to be published and got angry when it was delayed. I began to behave like all the others who call themselves a 'writer'. Who has shoulder-length hair, wears a black cravat and a wide-brimmed hat. Who makes friends with magazine editors in order to have a novella published every month. Who has a collection of poetry produced by a provincial printer, as well as a collection of short stories with a brightly coloured cover, who enters the Civil Service, marries and spends the rest of his life weighed down by a scraggy little wife and several badly brought-up children. I too have had my moment of glory. I've experienced the meagre satisfaction of having an article published on the front page, without spelling mistakes, my name beneath the title...

And I've stooped even lower. I got a tailor to make me some 'modern' clothes. I've started wearing silk socks, I've regretted not having longer hair, I've used talcum powder just like Dinu, I too have read the latest French novels and literary magazines, I too have gone to the cinema, and – after every defeat – my friends, my good friends, all assure me that I'm becoming civilized, that I'm almost 'normal'.

So I can't blame myself for wasting an entire afternoon standing in the corner, staring at the sky and thinking about my sorrows. It simply had to happen.

Night is drawing in. My memories have driven away the melancholy. I'll be able to read without fear of spending a whole hour on one page. I'm feeling calm and depressed. There's a void in my soul that no human will can fill. It would be futile to even try.

VI

Rehearsals

Rehearsals for *A Model Lycée* have begun. We meet every evening in the music room. The director is Mr Filimon from the National Theatre. Mr Filimon directs all the plays that we put on for school festivals. He knows the boys and enjoys their company. He smokes all the time, gives us friendly taps on the shoulder and secretly tells us little anecdotes. Anecdotes that, he hastens to add, shouldn't be repeated at home or in class.

The masters warmed to the idea of Fănică's 'variety show'. About ten days ago we all got together in the music room at the end of school. The Headmaster was there, smiling and frowning, depending on the circumstances. The other professors sat in the front row, making a lot of noise and smoking as they waited to hear a read-through of the show. Fănică, who was red in the face because of his tight collar and anxiety, stood next to the piano. I was going to accompany him. On a small table nearby he had put a pile of musical scores that I had to decipher. There were ballads, modern dances, marches and couplets.

I began to play. Fănică hummed along, his voice quavering. He simplified the tenor parts or dropped an octave.

The masters listened very closely, captivated, while the Headmaster kept looking at them one by one, trying to establish what attitude he ought to take towards the pupil Bănăţeanu Ştefan's variety show. The masters encouraged him.

Then Fănică explained the show to them: 'The man-about-town boys each sing a verse in the Headmaster's study'

Filled with curiosity, the Headmaster asked: 'And I gave them permission to sing to me?'

'Oh, no! You won't be in your study at the time.'

'So where will I be?'

'Teaching a class.'

Finally the Headmaster understood. He smiled. Fănică – as nervous as he was in trigonometry lessons – went on: '...And then suddenly you walk into your study. You find them singing and dancing, you get angry and shout: 'What are you doing in here? What sort of uniforms do you call these? Why is your hair so long? Where are the numbers on your tunics?'

Fănică did his best to imitate the Headmaster when he was in a rage. The Headmaster was flattered. He laughed, supporting his belly with one hand. – a gesture left over from when he was wounded in the war.

Verse after verse, dialogue after dialogue, the masters approved of everything.

'We now have the verses sung by the pupil who caught jaundice in a chemistry class.

Knowing glances between Fănică and Toivinovici. The masters roared with laughter and smoked away contentedly. Before he began, Fănică asked me to give him the note. I played three white keys, one after another. Then six opening bars. It's a very well known tune that can be heard every summer at the Cărăbus Theatre. The lively rhythm of the verses won them over. Fănică was overflowing with enthusiasm. He tapped his foot in time with the music. After every verse he paused to explain.

'Now the master sings...'

Toivinovici went bright red. Who knows what was going through his mind at this point.

And then the pupil sings:
'Every night I leap out of bed,
a question buzzing round my head:
What is alcohol,
What is phenol,
Or benzine
glycerine
stearin,

paraffin,
phosphates
and hydrates,
What's with this chlorine,
or vitriol,
and oxine,
and amine,
oxygen,
hydrogen,
sulphite,
cuprite,
fructose
glucose,
apatite,
galalith...
Whether I'm alive or dead,
they'll still be buzzing round my head'.

The masters didn't object to anything in Act I. Act II, however, with its triumphal march and the protest against the 'Lalescu Scale' gave them something to think about. But Fănică carried it off yet again. The masters laughed at any verses that made fun of their colleagues. And so in the end, everyone had his share of satisfaction and resentment.

The Headmaster decided that we could begin rehearsing. The masters all lit cigarettes, and left the music room, offering Fănică their congratulations. Fănică wiped his forehead with a handkerchief, because he wasn't a tenor.

The other boys, who were waiting outside in the courtyard, greeted the news with great excitement. The minor roles were then distributed.

We get together in the music room. Apart from the 'actors', there are a few other boys who help us. Minculescu, from the Upper Sixth, was one of the first to volunteer. He has a large nose, but is very kind and gentle. And he's an outstanding prompter. Dinu, who is very keen to attend rehearsals, usually sits next to him. Petrişor,

Furtuneanu, Perri and various others also come. They stand at the back and comment on the different parts. They also give their views on how each of us will perform. For me they predict a great success.

Once everyone who is in the first scene has arrived, Mr Filimon claps his hands.

'Now then, gentlemen!'

Fosil plays the piano, and always looks bored. To spur him on, the other boys give him a nudge whenever they get the chance, and shout: 'Come on, Fosil!'

But the pianist complained to the director, and threatened to tell the Headmaster.

Gianni has difficulty moving around 'on stage'. Mr. Filimon sighs, wipes his glasses and taps his forehead in despair.

'No no no, Mr Gianni. You're far too stiff and starchy, old chap.'

Gianni blushes, because the audience on the benches are delighted. He sulks, and threatens not to play the part if people make 'all that racket.' These threats make Fănică uneasy. He trembles at the thought of his 'troupe' falling apart. He hastens to placate Gianni, and reassures him that his voice was becoming far more powerful and sonorous.

So Gianni sings:
'Every class is deadly dull
No matter who the master,
So here I sit as if 'en salon'
Reading lines from La Garçonne.'

When he finishes, the boys on the benches all applaud, Mr Filimon laughs in relieved delight, while the playwright bites his nails for fear that Gianni might pull out.

Then Mr Filimon claps his hands again.

'Come along now, gentlemen! Be more serious! Piano...'

Fosil heaves a sigh. The prompter finds the page. Boys from the junior forms jostle at the window to feast their eyes on the 'actors'. Fănică shoos them away in a most dignified fashion.

In the middle of a classroom, the four man-about-town boys dance and sing the chorus from the song *Machinalement*. Filimon beats time with his arms. The gym master, Mr Daian, smokes and hides his cigarette behind his back.

The director interrupts: 'There's just one thing that worries me. If you go on like that you'll trample on each others toes. Okay, one more time everyone!'

'They don't understand that after the war
We simply weren't the same any more.'

Someone shouts: 'That's actually rather good'.

Filimon interrupts: 'Do you mind. Let's leave the comments to the audience.'

Flattered, the audience burst out laughing.

We come to the scene with 'The angry father.' Angry because of the extra music and gym lessons that his son is forced to attend – almost every afternoon. 'The father' is played by Pake. He was a provisional choice. Because Pake's diction is not very good. And the director can't stand poor diction.

'Mr. Protopopescu!'

'I haven't got my part with me...'

Mr Filimon claps his hand to his forehead: 'Why don't you bring your *parts*, gentlemen? Why not, Mr Protopopescu? Why didn't you bring it, my dear boy?'

Fănică starts biting his nails again.

'Because I certainly gave you the part.'

'But how was I to know that there were rehearsals today?'

'How did everyone else know?'

Filimon gives up: 'Fine, let's make a start then. Mr Minculescu will prompt for you.

Minculescu nods his head in agreement.

The director gives the signal: 'Enter.'

Pake walks on stage, which is set up as a classroom.

'Good m-m-morning!'

'Not like that. Say "Good morning!" Louder, Mr Protopopescu! Louder, so we can hear you.'

'Here I am, M-M-Mr...'

'What was that? We can't hear a thing, my dear fellow. Not even from where I'm standing. Speak clearly, gentlemen.'

'B-B-But w-w-why all d-d-day, m-my g-g-good s-sir? Th-this is f-f-far t-too m-m-much. M-my s-s-son, who used to s-study n-nine hours a d-d-day, n-now s-studies only f-f-five, and g-got a s-second prize in stead of f-f-first . Pl-please, I ask y-you to excuse h-him!...'

'No, no, no, no!... Speak more slowly, my dear chap. Once again, please... Enter!'

'G-good m-morning, H-H-Headmaster...'

The audience laughs. Someone cracks a joke, and it's passed on along the benches. But Filimon hears, and gets annoyed: firstly because there's a rumpus, secondly because he can't think of an immediate response.

'Open your mouth more, Mr Protopopescu! If you articulate properly you'll be able to speak as quickly as you like.'

Silence. Pake repeats the line for the third time. It doesn't work, and the others are at their wits' end. Fănică tries to find someone else to play 'The angry father.' Pake, who has learnt his verse and the melody before anything else, makes a final effort to redeem himself.

'I'll sing my verse then.'

'Never mind the verse, old chap. You want to torment us with your verse now, do you?

Pake laughs.

Mr Boloveanu appears at the window, wearing his overcoat. He has come for the fanfare. Ever since we began our 'theatre rehearsals,' he hasn't had anywhere for the band to practice. In fact, the number of these gatherings has been reduced. The boys got bored with the fanfare. The only people who still come are from the junior forms, or those who still believed Mr Boloveanu's threats.

The theatre 'rehearsal' makes the Maestro feel more cheerful. He roars with laughter. And then he remembers why he's there, and tries to come to an arrangement with Mr Filimon. As he's doing so, he produces a piece of official school writing paper that bears the Headmaster's elaborate signature. It has to be signed by all the members of the band, who would thereby commit themselves to attending regular rehearsals and doing what Mr Boloveanu tells them.

Hardly anyone signs it. We produce ridiculous or non-existent excuses. A few people – the more mischievous ones – comment out loud so that Mr Boloveanu can hear.

Then Mr Filimon makes a general announcement: 'Gentlemen! Listen to me, my dear fellows. Pay attention to how you leave the stage, don't rush or you might miss the door. And don't trip over your feet! You'll ruin the whole effect with a poor exit. Believe me. Now we'll move on to the scene with the Director of Music and the gym master.'

The Headmaster – which is to say, Bricterian – calls for the school servant, Coteț[18], who is played by Vintilescu. This is because they're both from Severin county. The Headmaster rings. The servant enters: 'Please ask the music and gym masters to come to my study.'

These masters have been summoned in order to give the angry father more information about extra lessons.

The boys are tired. They lean against the walls and watch the antics of the director, the playwright and the music and gym masters. Nonetheless, some are still working. Gianni is 'rehearsing' his part with Morariu by dancing it. Fănică does his utmost to teach those who have difficult verses to learn. Occasionally he listens to them sing, and frowns when they make too many mistakes. Bricterian tries to play *The Ride of the Valkyires* on the organ, using one finger.

The happiest of all, however, is Robert. He walks round the room, tapping his feet to the rhythm of a dance that he has invented to go with the music for his verse, his head tilted to one side, arms swinging, eyes half closed. He's already savouring his glory, basking in the encores he'll get after the opening scene, just like he told us.

He stops in front of me, pats me on the shoulder and shares his latest secret: 'You know I've learnt the verse sung by the pupil who's just taken his Baccalaureate?'

'...'

'Pitch perfect. And I've sorted out my costume. Plus how I'm going to do my make-up. Dark eyes, red lips, a little rouge on my cheeks... I'll outshine everyone... the girls will have eyes for me alone.'

And that's not all. During the dress rehearsal he's going to practice casting roving looks into the private boxes while he's singing.

'That's what all the famous actors do. And after the performance I'll get billets-doux and declarations of love, I guarantee it.'

Silence. He looks me in the eye and smiles sweetly. Then he strokes my cheek.

'You're a hell of a good chap, doctor.'

We leave the rehearsal in groups. Filimon tells anecdotes and the boys all laugh uproariously, just to please him. Outside the gate we divide into three bigger groups. The man-about-town boys head towards the Calea Victoriei.

We actors don't have to worry about homework. The masters wouldn't dare test us. We lie when we tell them that we have rehearsals every day, all afternoon. So they spare us. They tell themselves that they each have someone to represent them on stage. That's what our teachers are like: decent people.

VII

The Road to Myself

I have to know myself. I have to know once and for all, and *for certain*, who I am and what I want. I've put this off time and time again because I was afraid. I was afraid I wouldn't be able to shine a light into my soul, or that the light would either pass over it or make me unhappy. I've imagined certain things about myself. But what if they don't really exist? What if they're just an illusion?

And that's not all. I've tried to live out the characteristics that I believe are part of my soul. I imposed them on myself, made them mine. What will happen to them if I discover that they're disguises that I've forced myself to wear? Will I be able to discard them without being overcome by the emptiness of my soul?

There have been many times when I've decided to analyse myself in depth, to calmly penetrate my soul as deeply as possible. But I haven't succeeded. I've never been able to concentrate. I wasn't able to think solely about myself. Every time I tried to analyse myself, I found myself in utter darkness. Where do I begin to look for myself? Where am I able to be myself?

What was I searching for? My soul. Where? And how would I be able to recognize my *real* soul among the thousands of souls that I seem to bear within me?

My mind began to wander. I woke up with my thoughts on other things. I tried again, stubbornly persisting, I closed my eyes, put my fingers in my ears, pressed my hands to my forehead. The same darkness. And nowhere did I encounter a single light, a single source of encouragement. How would I ever find myself? How would I ever find my soul and live according to its needs?

Because I want to know myself, so I can understand which path I have to follow.

I once wasted an entire afternoon and only discovered one thing, something I'd suspected for a long time: that the me of the present moment is not the same as the one from an hour ago, and even less so the one from yesterday. This left me totally astonished. I am now at a loss to understand why I decided to set out in search of my soul in the first place. If my soul isn't a single entity, but an infinity, how could I ever come to know the real one? I've noticed that running through these numerous states of consciousness there is a single, continuous line.

But I have my doubts about the reality of this continuous line, which would constitute a personality. It seems that the origin of this continuity might lie in my own will, or the suggestions made by the people around me. I've noticed that people try not to contradict what they or others believe about them. In which case, personality would simply be imposed by our will, and not something that springs from the depths of our soul. It would be nothing but a mask.

But I know that everything I've written up till now can't be true. I know there is such a thing as a single soul, and that it is reflected in thousands of fleeting viewpoints. That behind every conscious-ness lies this single soul. That there are many times when strange states of consciousness slip through, but they are temporary, and can be set aside by the simplest self-examination.

So I sense that within me there exists a single soul. But how do I go about reaching it? The task seems so impossible that it fills me with dread. If I were given an algebra or geometry question to solve – notwithstanding my shortcomings in maths – I'd be able to work it out, or at least identify the way in which this could be done. In the very worst case I would know where to start.

Yet when I try to find myself, I don't have any such method at my disposal, not even a clue. It's as if my self is a completely dif-ferent world. I tried to shed some light on the subject by reading psychology books, but couldn't find what I'm looking for. Such books discuss other subjects, no doubt interesting in themselves, but not the means by which I can come to know myself, and master the power of my soul.

And this is vital to me. Because otherwise I'll never have the courage to succeed in life. If I can't find the road that leads to my soul, I'm sure I'll perish.

My soul... this is what troubles me. I'm unable to draw it into the light. I'd like to come across my soul in the same way that I find a dog's pancreas in anatomy class. I'd like to measure it, weigh it, ascertain its value. I'd like to know if my soul is the soul of a melancholic adolescent or an over-excited male. If I am a man of learning, or a romantic. If I should trust in my current preoccupations, or if I should be suspicious, and fear changes that come too soon.

For there are days when my will is strong and my mind as clear as a grown man's. At these times I work relentlessly, plan what I'm going to read and make a list of my books.

But there are other days when I wake up late and come home from school disheartened, when everything around me seems dull and pointless. I hate these days most of all.

My eyes stray from the page, I keep wiping my glasses in order to kill time, and I wonder: what's the point? And if I look at the list of things that I plan to do, I feel sad.

And then there are the times that I spend staring out of my attic window, or wandering along unknown streets beneath the chestnut trees. These times trouble me, make me uneasy. Times when I don't recognize myself. When I'm harried by a single thought, and have to summon up all my willpower to chase it away. Otherwise my courage would desert me. And I ask myself: when I'm older, will I regret this foolish adolescence that I've lived on the margins of life? When I'm older, will I mourn the seventeen years that I am today, a day which, for me, will end in this attic, all alone, occasionally looking out of the window at two poplar trees?

I know I'm not good-looking, but I am seventeen. And at those moments when my eyes wander from my book and my will begins to weaken, I think a great deal about these seventeen years.

There are many times when I succeed. I work late into the night, and fall asleep with a smile on my lips, content in the knowledge that I've won a victory over myself. At other times, however, I'm unable to resist. And, overwhelmed, I head out into the street.

All this makes me sad. I have to be constantly engaged in a struggle, I have to defend myself against the soul that I don't know, and which sometimes reveals itself to me in a most contradictory way. My soul is never the same. Every day I encounter a different one. And I have to struggle to continue what I began a month ago, a week ago, a day ago.

If only I knew myself... then I would have so much more confidence in myself and my life... I would say: such is my soul, and that is how I like it to be. But for now I live in fear of the dark, forbidding future towards which I'm headed, guided by a blind soul. And what if at some later date everything becomes clearer, and I realize that I've taken the wrong path? Will I feel like a stranger in a world that I now regard as a friend? Will I have the courage to turn back, to start yet another new life? And will I have the strength?

More than once, while trying to discover who I am, I've been seized with dread. I wasn't able to recognize myself in many of the things I've said and done. It was as if it were *someone else*. Before going to sleep I would think about the day that had just gone by, almost without me knowing. And I would ask myself: which one was my soul? And then, much to my horror, many strange souls would appear before my eyes.

One day I discovered that the soul I believed was mine while I was reading was actually unknown to me. And I fell asleep, exhausted and despondent. At other times I would hurry home and set to work, the master of my thoughts and soul.

While walking down the street, I would hear, drifting out of open windows, the same scales and sonatas that I had been made to play many years ago, how I had cried because my fingers were too small or the octaves too wide. Or I would hear melodies that awoke feelings of sorrow and regret in my soul. And then my steps would falter. My soul had changed. I was disheartened. The thought of my little room with all its books would cease to spur me on. I would walk more and more slowly, take one detour after another before finally getting home, my mind empty of thoughts. Not of the precious hours that I had wasted under the chestnut trees. Nor even of the books that I would write.

There were days when I would be filled with sadness at the sight of some simple illustrations, the kind that litter the pages of magazines. A girl sitting on a bench under a leafy tree somewhere, and in the distance a line of hills that I could see were bathed in sunlight. This particular etching always made me sad whenever I studied it closely. I couldn't say exactly why. But there's such a look of melancholy in the girl's eyes as she sits there all alone under a leafy tree... and so many regrets in the line of hills that exists somewhere, not far away, but which I never look at because I walk straight past, my gaze fixed on a dead world.

There's another simple illustration that affects me in the same way. It shows a country road lined with poplar trees. In the fields, reapers are busy with the harvest. A man walks along the road. It's trite. Boring. And yet I always spend a long time looking at the poplars and the traveller. Perhaps I associate them with the poplars in the courtyard surrounded by the iron fence, which I can see from my attic window. I think of the fields that I only see in summer, or on Sundays in springtime, when I wander far from the city.

I hide the magazines and try to carry on reading. But I can't. I'm filled with remorse. I look out of the window and see the poplar trees, the leaden coloured roofs, hear the muffled sounds of the street. Sometimes night falls. I may have cried several times without realizing.

Wearily, I light the lamp.

And then the room comes to life again, the books speak to me from their shelves, my soul returns. And I always regret the time I wasted looking out of the window, or crying over a melody played on the piano and a drawing of a country road in summer.

I'd like to know who I am, because I don't know. I've filled a great many notebooks trying to find out, but I haven't succeeded. My novel is going to be full of strange heroes. Their souls won't be one-dimensional, or all of a piece. Up till now I've never met an adolescent with a soul like this. But I won't be able to analyse my characters because I've never met them. So I won't be able to plumb the depths of their souls.

I look at myself. Deep down within. So many odd characteristics, so many contradictions.

That's why I'll never be able to write *The Novel of the Short-Sighted Adolescent*, which is the only hope I've got.

VIII

Incipit Vita Nova

It snowed all day. My soul would probably have liked to feel sad, but I wouldn't let it. That's why I was happy today, because it was how I wanted to be. I read late into the night. And then, exhausted, I began to ask myself questions. Autumn is over, and many of the things that I promised myself I would achieve, I've left half-completed. I've written less and less frequently in this notebook, and taken it less and less seriously. I haven't analysed myself. And I haven't studied psychology to help me understand myself.

Other ideas have occurred to me. I've begun to enjoy other things. Rarely do I think about chemistry. I'd really like to know what the soul is, but I think it's extremely difficult to understand. I've read many books, but gained nothing from them: quite the opposite. So now I want to read Bergson.

At least I've escaped mathematics, which is something to be happy about. I had to make a decision to change to the Humanities. And so I did. They let me take the preliminary exam in May. And then I was given the Latin texts that are used in the Remove and the Fifth Form.

The atmosphere in the Humanities is completely different. The master is lenient, erudite and ironic. He tells us a lot of things that we then discuss among ourselves. But he despises our ignorance. This 'Maestro' of ours is an occultist and a philosopher. That's why he spends so little time on grammar, preferring to improve our use of logic and the quality of our knowledge. He enjoys listening to us discuss a topic, and then delights in exposing the holes in our arguments.

Up till now I haven't done much Latin. So I had to start from scratch, with *aquila, aquilae*, and then all the way up to Caesar.

Yet at the moment I'm translating Horace. I bought some cloth-bound texts with cardboard covers. I've read all the introductions. I really like the Latin language, and the masters, the authors we study, and our class.

Since the 'Maestro' only sets an exam at the end of the year and doesn't give us written homework or surprise tests, we spend virtually the entire time discussing the subject, or doing the occasional short commentary on a text. This is why we all pay attention. Because we don't live in fear of marks, reports or snap tests. The mainstays of our discussions are usually Leiber and Petrişor. Whenever Leiber translates and comments on a text, Petrişor stands up and criticizes. Once Petrişor has finished, Leiber gets up to defend himself. They toss ironic remarks back and forth. The rest of us prefer Petrişor's irony, although the 'Maestro' has his doubts about both of them.

Fănică sits in the second row. He has covered all his textbooks with blue paper, and writes all his Latin vocabulary in a special notebook. Next to him is Brătăşanu. Brătăşanu is brilliant at grammar. Even the 'Maestro' himself once told him: 'You'll addle your brains, old chap!'

Brătăşanu knows all the irregular verbs and can translate any text. He doesn't even have to look at the book, he only has to listen to the phrase. But he doesn't understand how Augustus became emperor, or why Horace wrote *Carmen Saeculare*. In the same way, to him all poets are 'marvellous.' When he has to comment on: '*Vides ut alta stat nive candidum Soracte...*' he tells us about Socrates, or the climate in Rome. Brătăşanu knows all the consuls, and their respective dates, from Tacitus's *Histories*. He studies the Varemberg dictionary and Saglio. But for all that he's no scholar. He forgets almost everything that he takes on board. Latin grammar and German vocabulary are the only things he doesn't forget. Brătăşanu knows an incredible amount of German words, and yet he can't read a German book without using a dictionary.

He's good at trigonometry, chemistry, physics, and zoology. Brătăşanu knows everything that a model pupil needs to know. That's why he's been top of the class and won all the prizes from the moment he arrived at the lycée. But actually – this is what I think – he doesn't know anything at all. All he knows is *what he's taught.*

He's popular because he's 'a good boy,' and will gladly come to your house to help you with Latin grammar and not ask for payment. After which he'll stay up after midnight doing his 'homework.' And he really does do it. He learns everything that he's given to learn, even when the 'homework' isn't very interesting and he knows he won't be tested on it. He's so conscientious it makes you sick. For written tests he revises absolutely everything. Because written tests – so Brătășanu tells us – are based on the whole term's work. Which is perfectly true. But I've never seen a good test essay produced by Brătășanu. He only ever repeats what he's read or heard the master say. He's not capable of anything else.

He's the class 'prefect.' He's also the monitor for the Humanities. Which is to say that he sits at the master's desk and threatens people: 'Marcu, I'm going to write your name in my book!'

When he isn't reading a novel, Marcu is the laziest and most disruptive person in the class. And yet – although he despises Latin civilization, which he regards as 'despotic' – he actually knows far more about it than the rest of us. He has read all of Tacitus, something that even the best pupils haven't done. Plus he's read several volumes of Boissier, which is something else that virtually no one else can claim. But Marcu isn't good at grammar, and produces poor translations. Given half a chance, he *cribs*. Whenever there's an oral exam he revises a few random paragraphs from the line-by-line translation. Which is why he always gets an 'Unsatisfactory' in Latin. But he's never made to retake, because the 'Maestro' doesn't allow this: 'I know that none of you ever do any work.'

Robert sits in the middle of the classroom, next to Bricterian. Robert can't translate, and hasn't read many books about Rome. But he knows how to talk. He talks whenever and about whatever comes into his mind. Not because he's talented, but because he thinks he 'speaks well.' At least that's Robert's opinion. Which is why he smiles and gives a little cough whenever he stands up. And then he starts talking. Slowly and melodically (or so he says), searching for his words, and then, once he finds them, pronouncing them triumphantly. He's very loquacious, because it means he can talk for longer. Even so, the boys say that last summer he gave quite a successful talk on *Circus Games in Ancient Rome*. The 'Maestro' congratulated him, and predicted that one day he'd be a great writer and orator. Robert blushed and strutted about self-importantly, barely saying a word to the rest of us. Yet his talk happened purely by chance. It was only a success because it came after Brătăşanu's, who spoke about *Roman Roads and Aqueducts*, summarizing a hundred pages in *quarto* from Varemberg and Saglio. Meanwhile the other boys played nine men's morris or backgammon. The 'Maestro' closed his eyes and nodded off. The only sounds were the speaker's voice and flies buzzing. When the bell rang, everyone gave a sigh of relief. Salvation at last! But Brătăşanu hadn't finished his talk on *Aqueducts*. And he never did finish, because the other boys wouldn't let him. And the next day it was Robert's turn.

Before the 'Maestro' arrives, Brătăşanu coaches people in Latin grammar and translation. At the same time, three rows back, Leiber does commentaries. Leibner's commentaries are original and very instructive – at least, for those who haven't read *La Cité antique*.* Because when it comes to 'the Ancient World', Leiber's erudition – rather like Brătăşanu's – is nothing but a myth. The night before a lesson, Leiber reads Fustel de Coulanges[19], so that the next day he is able to quote Latin authors and sources that he's never set eyes on.

Leiber always 'speaks' after Robert has finished, and criticizes him in scholarly fashion. Petrişor, meanwhile, smiles ironically. Naturally, once Leiber has talked himself hoarse, Petrişor stands up. He doesn't know much about 'the Ancient World' either, but his job is to criticize Leiber. Whatever Leiber says, we can be sure that Petrişor won't agree. Quite the opposite. Nonetheless, the truth is always on Petrişor's side.

The rest of the class are always delighted when a discussion between the 'orators' begins to get heated. Mişu Tolihroniade is another of the 'orators', although he doesn't say as much. When he does stand up, he goes red and speaks very precisely. Most of the time he smiles ironically, in order to 'baffle' his opponent.

My classmates in the Humanities are a very engaging crowd. I've become friends with quite a lot of them. There's no doubt that the Humanities are far superior to the Sciences. Mainly because of Vanciu, the atmosphere there was frosty. The people who were good at maths could eat croissants until Vanciu walked in. But as for the rest of us...

That's why I'm happy. So I ought to forget all the sadness that the snowy days have brought me. I have a good companion in Horace.

IX

Christmas Eve

The choir meets in my attic every evening. To give us more light we take the globe off the lamp. We smoke and enjoy ourselves chatting while we wait for everyone to arrive. We discuss the rehearsals for *A Model Lycée* and gossip about Robert. We all take unusual delight in gossiping about Robert. Because ever since he told us that it won't be long before he wins the love of a princess, he's become quite unbearable.

We're all good friends. We call each other by our first names, swear at each other without causing offense, lend each other money and share confidences about our 'conquests.' Every night, Poprişan – who is a bass and lives in the suburbs, in Floreasca – tells us about a woman who's in love with him, sparing no details. He claims that she's 'hysterical,' and we listen to him, because that's what friends are for.

Fănică is keen to find out about certain establishments. He's a serious boy. As far as I know, he's never wanted to get involved with 'hysterical' women. He prefers to pay a fixed amount of money every week, and avoid any problems. His main interests are chemistry and maths, which is enough to put off Robert, who will soon win the love of a princess.

Other friends soon arrive, – tenors, baritones, basses – who admire my books and my perseverance. They all tell me the same thing: that they wouldn't have my 'willpower'. For my part I'm flattered, try to be modest and give them a pat on the back.

One or two of the 'elite' ask me what I'm writing at the moment, and who publishes my work. I'm sure that none of them have read a word of anything I've written. Because it wouldn't 'interest' them. Although they admire my boxes of insects, which astonish them.

They're amazed at how many I have, and that their legs are all intact. So I explain that I preserve them in a solution of sublimate then pin them on a piece of cork to dry. They all ask what the greenish-gold beetles in the corner are called. And I calmly tell them: *Cetonia aurata*. This impresses them.

Fănică is only sorry that I have so few butterflies and so many 'bees.' Three of my other friends think the same. I tell them that they aren't bees, they're Hymenoptera. But as we haven't yet learnt about insects in zoology, Fănică has no way of knowing this. He still insists that butterflies are more 'beautiful', and more interesting.

'I see them differently.'

There are too many of us to get involved in heated discussions about literature and philosophy. That's what we usually talk about late into the evening when it's just Bricterian, Petrişor, Dinu and myself. Bricterian paces up and down as he speaks. As my attic is very small, this doesn't calm him down, but only makes him more agitated.

Dinu sits in the armchair, smoking as he talks. When he gets angry, he sits up and speaks more loudly.

Petrişor argues like a sophist. All this achieves is to annoy the rest of us, because we're not in a position to refute his sophisms with logic.

We begin rehearsals, with Fănică conducting. Perri has lent him a tuning fork. Fănică gives it a mighty tap against the edge of the desk, closes his eyes and begins: *laaaa...* the tuning fork is indispensable, as is his reed baton.

First we sing *Bună Dimineaţa la Moş-Ajun*[20] with three voices. The tenors open their mouths as wide as possible, and throw their heads back. The basses clamp their lips together and lower their chins onto their chests. They say that's how the choir sings at the Patriarchate.

Fănică is happy with *Bună Dimineaţa*. We're all red in the face, and wipe our foreheads with our handkerchiefs, very pleased with ourselves. After that we sing *The leaves on the vine have turned to gold*, which, as Fănică explains, is no longer very popular, except in old folks' homes. Then comes *A student's life for me*, which makes us feel sad, and reminds Bricterian of Heidelberg of old. We also practice *On our standard is writ the word United*, for singing at patriots' houses. And *In all Seville there is none like you*, a romantic ballad from *Don Juan*. This is Robert's favourite. He says that we 'don't really understand it.' And he half closes his eyes and smiles. Some people look at him admiringly. He runs his fingers through his cropped hair and sighs: 'I'm in love with a woman...'

Fănică reminds him that we also need to practice *Gaudeamus igitur*. So Robert resigns himself. The others are keen to perform this student hymn and sing solemnly, despite not knowing the words and straining to hear the person next to them: '...ita nostra, ă, evis est.'

'evis... iii, eretur...'

Fănică does his best to pronounce the words as clearly as possible so the tenors can hear. But they're completely carried away and have stopped listening to the conductor.

Finally we rehearse *Many Years* and *Let us drink our whole life through as I drink wine today with you*. We sing these because we know we'll be invited into some of our friends' houses and need to be prepared. We'll leave our coats in the cloakroom, smile politely and peel our mandarins. There will be young ladies who will tell us: 'Please, help yourselves!'

And the ladies will admire us: 'How long have you been rehearsing?'

And then Bricterian will be asked to sing the prologue from *Pagliaccio*, and he'll say that he's slightly hoarse, and give a meaningful cough.

But in the end he'll give in:

'*Si puo, si puo, Signore, Signori;*
Scusatemi. Se da sol mi presento:
Io sono il prologo...'

The young ladies will fall in love with him, and his friends will pat him on the back and say: 'You're quite good for an Armenian.'

The night was clear and cold. The light covering of snow had frozen and was glittering. The boys arrived in groups, and greeted each other heartily at the door to my attic: 'Salve, Babo!'

'Hurrah, old chap!'

'Here you are...'

Fănică asked if anyone had been eating nuts or had drunk red wine. For those who broke the rules, he fixed a scale of punishment. For a minor misdemeanour it was a twenty lei fine, deducted from the money we would be paid at the end. A more serious offence would mean missing the choir feast, or permanent expulsion. Fănică is a little tyrant. But these are only threats. The rules are a mere formality.

We set off at quarter past nine. Altogether there were fifteen boys. Eleven choir members, a conductor, a treasurer and two 'kibitzers'. In the courtyard we sang for Mama. She listened at the window, smiling. Then she gave us mandarins, figs, biscuits, apples, and slipped the treasurer a banknote. Everyone said '*Sărut-mâna*[21]'and wondered: 'How much did she give us?'

Then we sang carols. We walked down the middle of the road, looking at each other, very pleased with ourselves and shouting: 'Gosh, there's so many of us!'

And we burst out laughing.

We walked into a courtyard surrounded by iron railings, where there were chestnut trees. A dog started barking, and then the lights suddenly went out. Fănică whistled through his teeth: 'Damn and blast!'

The boys were disgusted. They swore at the owners and walked out, slamming the gate behind them.

At the next house we were made welcome. We sang *Bună Dimineața...* out of tune, then *In all Seville...* and then *A student's life for me*. Then we waited. And then we sang again *Many Years*. A woman with a bright, cheerful face came out and asked how much we had in our wallet. We took this as a joke and roared with laughter, although we could have got away with just smiling.

On her tray were all the traditional fruits. The boys walked over sheepishly, and took the first thing they laid hands on. By the time I got there, there was nothing left except five nuts and a fig. I took them and thanked the woman politely.

Once we were out the gate, the treasurer told us: 'A hundred lei!'

At a large house in Batiştei Street, the gate was padlocked. At another, the lights went out the moment we launched into: '*Bună Dimineaţa la Moş-Ajun...*'

Poprişan picked up the metal shoe-scraper from outside the door, dragged it across the courtyard and threw it over the fence.

'...Bloody upstarts! That'll teach you to turn the lights out!'

And then he shouted, loud enough to be heard inside the house: 'What do you think, you tight-arsed sods! That we're starving to death and came to beg? Never heard of tradition? Merry Christmas to you too!'

Fănică would have stopped him, but he was laughing up his sleeve and couldn't control himself. We quickly slunk back out into the street, where our courage returned. Some people were offended by Poprişan's vernacular, while others enjoyed it.

We wandered along several other streets. Every now and then, when we got to a crossroads, we heard male voices, and would stop to listen. We agreed that none of the other choirs were a patch on ours.

When we got to Radu's house, we hung our coats in the cloak-room and crowded into the dining room, where we were served tea. In crystal fruit bowls on the table were mandarins and shiny apples. With tea there was rich fruit cake, and those of us who hadn't had supper were delighted. We felt constantly obliged to be witty. The target of all our jokes was Robert, along with a few of the others. But Radu was spared.

We sang.

'*Let us drink our whole life through as I drink wine today with you!*'

Some people put in: '*Just a drop!*'

While others responded, lowering their voices: '*Drink up! Drink up!*'

This always managed to raise our spirits. As we sang we smiled, our faces shining.

We left Radu's as soon as his mother had given us a hundred lei, and gathered up all the apples and oranges that were left on the table. The cake had been finished long ago.

At about eleven o'clock we were invited into a very grand house. We sang as beautifully as we could. And had another success with

Oarsmen, the night is falling. Our audience seemed very pleased as they nibbled biscuits in front of us. When we'd finished they asked if that was all we could sing, and when we assured them that it was, they gave us forty lei.

So as we left, we took the steel cannon balls from outside the front door and carried them down the street. This took some of the sting out of the insult, and calmed us down somewhat.

At midnight, seeing that there were now very few houses with lights on, we decided to stop. We headed back to my place, where a feast was waiting for us, including bottles of wine. On the way we called in at Fănică's, where we picked up five bottles of wine as well as some money. Robert had also given us some wine, but we had drunk it all as we went round. Fănică's warnings had been in vain. No one was afraid of being fined anymore.

'We're freezing, boss!'

'If we could just warm up a bit, we'd sing better, Fănică.'

'If not we'll get hoarse...'

'And then there'll be no tenors.'

When we arrived, Mama had laid the table in the attic.

The boys were more than a little pleased with the turkey, the wine, and the atmosphere. Some of them, who were tired, went into the next room to smoke. Baba and Poprişan opened the bottles and tried to get Brătăşanu drunk. He had brought a bottle of liqueur that he had distilled himself, and a bag full of little glasses. He poured some for us and said the liqueur was excellent. But no one was able to finish their glass, because it was far too sweet. Brătăşanu suddenly became very talkative, and started waving his arms about. The boys couldn't resist the temptation to get him drunk. They poured him one glass after another, and said: 'Here's to you, boss.'

'The boss' downed it triumphantly and gave a sigh: 'No more.'

'Don't be such a baby, boss.'

'I've had enough.'

'Nonsense! Only three glasses.'

'I think you're scared...'

'No I'm not.'

'Then drink this.'

'I can't.'

'You're not serious, boss?'

'Drink it before it gets warm.'

'I can't drink another drop.'

'What a baby!'

'Do it for me...'

'Tut-tut!'

'Leave him alone, he's scared...'

'Are you scared of getting drunk?'

'But who's going to see you?'

They put the glass to his lips, and the boss suddenly found his resolve. He took the glass and downed it in one. Then he turned an even brighter shade of red and just managed to say: 'I can't drink anymore.'

In the next-door room, the others wondered 'how it was going.'

Some people were certain that in a quarter of an hour he'd be 'plastered.' They made suggestions.

'You should replace the wine with...'

'Pour a glass of rum into the bottle.'

But then events took an unexpected turn. Brătășanu tore himself away from Poprișan's and Baba's clutches, and swore that he wouldn't touch another drop of wine all night. And then he promptly gathered up his glasses, asked if we had enjoyed the liqueur, and said: 'I'm off.'

The boys all gathered round him: 'Where are you off to?'

'Stay! We're going to Madame Roza's...'

'Girls! You know!'

But Brătășanu put his glasses in the bag, shook a few hands and then staggered to the door. At which point the boys began to sing:

When I drink another short,
I don't give poverty a thought.
When I'm flat out on the floor
My ailments are no more.

Brătășanu thanked them, but wouldn't change his mind about going home.

'But why are you going?'

'Because I want to.'

'Why do you want to?'

'It's a secret.'

'Never mind her, you can see her tomorrow.'

'It's Christmas Eve.'

'We're all going to Madame Roza's.'

Then someone said, reprovingly: 'Leave him alone boys, you're making him blush.'

Brătăşanu protested: 'I'm not blushing, I know all about that.'

'If you know, why don't you want to come?'

'Because.'

So we let him go. Brătăşanu set off alone through the snow, trying to look impassive.

The rest of us stayed in the attic for quite a while. We ate all the food and drank most of the wine. The room soon got so full of smoke that we had to open the windows.

When we finally decided to leave, it was half-past four in the morning.

We went outside and wandered down the street together for quite a while, laughing and joking. But after much deliberation, we decided that it was too late to go Madame Roza's.

So we all wished each other 'Merry Christmas', and promised to meet up again at Fănică's house on the third day of Christmas, which was his birthday. Then we all went our separate ways. Dinu and I walked home together, singing:

Ride a white horse, ride a white horse,
With a green saddle cloth (repeat).
O, keep me on her back, Lord, keep me on her back,
Don't let me tumble off (repeat).

PART III

I

Saturday

I have to write about this: we look forward to Saturday as a special day. Not because it is followed by Sunday, but because Saturday is the day of the body. Robert would call it the day of love. And Poprişan, the day of hysterical women.

Yet the truth is quite different. On Saturday nights we make our way to houses with red lanterns, where we find neither love nor hysterical women.

At our age we regard it as a duty. Anyone who tries to wheedle out of it becomes the target of shameful accusations. Houses with red lights are gymnasiums where masculine prowess is revealed and nurtured. There are exams to pass here as well, bringing with them the same fits of nerves that torment the soul and cloud the mind. And they're just as necessary as other exams.

Since we lack the personal charm, time and money, we don't try to 'conquer' the women. That rarely happens in any case. Using the little money we have, we just buy the quarter of an hour that the act of love requires. Which could be regarded as rather sad.

Perhaps our adolescent imaginations had conjured up faces other than the ones we saw leering at us after midnight. Perhaps we would have liked to hold a body tightly in our arms, to sink our teeth into lips. Perhaps we dreamt of women with dark, smouldering eyes – the sort you find in books – who would enslave our souls and slip into our bedroom at night. But the years went by, and the women of our dreams had still to cross our path. They still hadn't stared deep into our eyes and stirred our blood. They still hadn't held themselves against us, ardent and spiteful. They hadn't whispered words from books or dreams in our ears. They hadn't kissed us long and hard, their lips crushed breathlessly against our own, their eyelids half-closed. All that was left to us were vague, unsettling hallucinations that we stored away deep down inside us, and which we could call upon to comfort us whenever we were sad or alone.

Instead we grew accustomed to gingerly caressing spent, exhausted bodies, kissing shoulders that smelt of cheap powder and eau de cologne. It wasn't easy to get used to. On our first visit we walked nervously into the cobbled courtyard. We went over to the windows, doing our best to put on a brave smile. What confronted us was withered bodies, hollow cheeks, dull eyes, rouge-smeared lips. We were tempted by obscene, chopped meat. Legs were exposed for us, while through translucent blouses we glimpsed soft, wilted shapes. Mouths smiled at us, a service that was included in the price of the body. For us they spoke aphrodisiac words that were drowned out by the cracked laughter of a drunken virgin...

I don't know about the others. And I don't want to know about them in the pages of this notebook, which must remain mine alone. All I remember is my night, my love; the body that gave itself to me at the price laid down by the local tariff.

I too had to take this step. And I did so, forcing myself to appear calm and dignified. I walked into the courtyard with the other three, who were familiar with the house and its 'girls.' I laughed, even though I was trembling. I wasn't trembling for fear of revealing my own body, but for fear of the strange women to whom I would have to speak, the banknotes I would have to leave on the table 'afterwards'.

Several men were standing staring in the window, their expressions either radiant or rapacious. And I stared too, along with the rest. Then I chose a body. A painfully short dress, without sleeves. Young cheeks. A low voice. I gestured to her, tapped on the window and smiled. She smiled back. The others congratulated me on my choice. They described the various delights that the 'girl' would offer me in exchange for two banknotes. Then they followed me to the door, full of boisterous humour and advice.

For a moment or two I was alone in the room, and looked round at the pictures, which were in poor taste, a lamp covered in flimsy red paper, and the bed.

The 'girl' came back. She locked the door and walked over to me with an affected, cat-like grace. I played my part and pretended to take her seriously. But then she told me that I was 'good-looking'. This was discouraging: I know myself, and I'm not 'good-looking'. I'm not ashamed of it, but I realized the 'girl' was lying, and hadn't even bothered to look at me properly.

She asked me what I was called. I don't like it when strangers want to know my name. I don't want to be recognized in public, or bask in the fame that comes with a handshake. Which is why I gave her a strange, foreign name. The 'girl' smiled at me.

What followed was devoid of emotion on either side. Deep down inside, however, I was still very uneasy. I couldn't wait for my companion to unlock the door and say 'good night'. Nervously, I put the money on the table then hurried over to the mirror. I didn't want to look her in the eye. She didn't seem to appreciate my sensitivities. She just counted the money, pulled up her dress and stuffed the notes into the top of her stocking.

Once I was outside, I came back down to earth. So *this* was love? The body? Women?

I wanted to spit and weep, to smash my fists against the railings. I was disgusted and humiliated. It was possibly the only time that I haven't dismissed suicide as contemptible. I wanted to run away, tear off the clothes that still smelt of cheap flesh, to forget the words I had spoken, our embraces on the bed.

But the others seemed satisfied with my show of nerve. They showered me with praise, said I would go far in life. Then we went to a bar and ordered drinks. Since I was the man of the moment, it was my round. My friends kept laughing and joking about 'the girl', and my melancholy state. They told me I ought to be glad. And that I was no longer a child. But I had already realized that.

I walked home alone, long after midnight. At one point I caught myself strutting like a peacock. I laughed under my breath. It meant that I was feeling more self-confident. And I was overjoyed.

But in the depths of my soul I was still filled with the same despair that I had felt when I looked at the girl with the money tucked in her stocking.

*

The months went by, and Saturday became gradually less exciting. The act was performed correctly, like an order that must be obeyed. Those of us who didn't make 'conquests' submitted to it without the slightest regret. At certain times of night we would walk into certain hidden courtyards where we made our selection.

Not a trace of sentimentality or sensuality. That only happens in books or to boyars' sons. But we poor intellectual boys man-handled all this chosen flesh simply to calm our nerves and clear our minds. Why hide it? Our love is purely functional. We don't engage in sexual perversions. We don't seek the sensual delights that appear on the price list. What would be the point? It would entice us into a whole new world, one that we couldn't and didn't wish to be acquainted with.

Some of my classmates fell in love during the school holidays. They loved and suffered for it. But it didn't last long. They stand around on the sidelines of love, but consider themselves dupes if they don't get French kisses and long embraces. So it comes down to functionality.

At parties we dance. These dances aren't artistic. Still less are they romantic. Bodies draw closer, take on a certain symmetry, and then they spin round and round in time with the music. This creates tensions on both sides. In other words, it's functionality.

Moralists might find all this annoying. But it exists. For a whole host of reasons we are unable to satisfy our sensual or romantic urges. Layer by layer they accumulate in our souls, where they sit and wait. Or mutate into strange, unexpected forms. Or become depraved and terrifying.

Perhaps I should write about these things with more warmth. Perhaps I should try to shed some light on what lies beneath them. But in my eyes it seems natural, and that's enough for me.

*

Having closely observed my friends and classmates for my 'novel,' I know for certain that none of them have ever made a single 'conquest.' Not Dinu, not Robert. Everything they say on the subject is a lie that the whole class accepts, although no one believes a word of it.

So it's simply functionality, with a price attached. Which is for the best. It's one more step towards understanding reality. Frequenting houses with red lights helps us acquire the qualities required to become conscientious, discriminating citizens. Which can only be cause for rejoicing.

Almost without realizing, those of us who are able to possess a body in exchange for two small blue banknotes, develop a quite different way of seeing women. These opinions may be far from the truth, but they are ours, not borrowed. They are imposed on us by life.

We always evaluate the bodies of women we see in the street from a purely obscene and financial viewpoint. Our eyes inspect every limb, and then fix a price in blue banknotes. We compare how much each of us would be prepared to pay for instant possession. If we have the time, the discussion often lasts for hours.

On Saturdays I always meet up with Marcu. We decide what we're going to do according to the time and money we have available. We might go to the cinema, or buy some toffee and go for a stroll in the Cişmigiu Gardens, where we have a discussion.

My discussions with Marcu are lively and impassioned, because he always contradicts me. I enjoy this, at least at the start.

We discuss a book we've been reading, or Cocea's latest article in *Facla*[22], or our favourite subjects. He tells me about anarchistic texts, while I initiate him into Orientalism. Since we have completely opposite opinions we're inseparable. He's a sceptic, I'm dogmatic. He's a materialist, I'm a victim of metaphysics. He's calm and affects an air of cold indifference, while I'm an uncontrollable torrent.

We walk side by side in the darkness, wracking our brains. And only our brains. Occasionally we discuss women, love, and bodies. But we do so in the light of intelligence, on which we pride ourselves. Deep down we're incurable romantics. We both realize this. And – being aware of our vulnerability – we do our best to conceal it.

Late at night we arrive at the houses, already knowing which faces we will see and which words we will hear. We go in. We notice unusual things. We observe the other visitors. We whisper our most valuable observations to each other. We double-check our impressions. We continue the discussion that we started an hour earlier, dissect it and struggle to find explanations and conclusions for these new situations. Everything around us is raw material to be collected, sifted and weighed. Neither of us is pedantic, nor do we feign exaggerated intellectualism, but these places and people are too tempting by far. Our brains, accustomed to asking questions, instinctively produce answers that demand justification.

At midnight comes the time for erotic overtures and accomplishments. We always take our time before choosing the 'girls.' Not because we want to pick the best goods, but because we wish to look at them for as long as possible out of pure curiosity.

*

In a room with an icon and many chairs, the girls sit and wait. Youthful or withered bodies, slender or stout. Bedroom attire, brightly coloured, short, transparent. Much-handled flesh at rest. Soft arms drape over the backs of chairs or hang heavily by their sides. Sterile hips that look inanimate, turned to stone. An impression of bones overheated by work, muscles left exhausted, blood grown turbid. Shoulders still bearing the imprint of the hands that coveted them. Large, round breasts hang shapeless.

But the wait doesn't last for long. Through the window, male eyes evaluate and choose. Features lit up by the nearby lamp, the girls study the group of men, and smile. With every gesture they hope to acquire a new client. This gives them new life. They deploy the last of their personal charms, which have so far remained hidden. Brazenly they stretch out their legs, uncover their thighs up to the hip. Then they fix their eyes on the men and wait for the sign.

Every now and then, one of the lucky ones comes back into the room, smiling. An old woman who sits in the corner making coffee gives her a kindly, consoling look. The others continue searching for partners among the group of men outside the window.

When we decide, the girls quickly get up and come and join us in the courtyard. Smilingly, they entice us into rooms with heavy curtains, from where we emerge satisfied, with slow, assured movements and brightly glowing cheeks.

And then we leave the courtyards and their red-lit lanterns, and make our way back along the same old streets, deep in discussion. We discuss with the same passion as before. The memory of the red lights doesn't make us quiver in the least. We don't bewail the fate of those bodies in transparent clothing. We shed not a tear over the injustice of the world. We walk on into the night, unflinching, and feel fresh blood pulsing through our veins.

*

But there are days when the streets are bathed in sunlight, and our bodies crave other bodies.

Why not admit it? Many a time I stare voraciously at hips and breasts hidden beneath clothing. I've inhaled the scent of a woman, my eyes glazed. In the tram and at the library I've imagined caressing the flesh of the temptress sitting next to me. I've wandered through dubious places, far off the beaten track. I've lusted after legs and white shoulders. I would have sunk my teeth into depraved, curling lips gulped down the trickling blood as if it were a rare and precious drink.

I'm ugly and morose. I hurry scowling though the streets, a suspicious look on my face. I'm afraid of attracting attention to myself too soon. The day will come when I will walk down the street with the light of victory shining from my eyes. But for now, I'm frightened. And scowling makes me even uglier. Beneath my half-closed eyelids, my eyes cloud over.

Bewitching bodies appear on every street corner. Fragile bodies, enticing bodies – mignon, shy, hypocritical – or tall, proud, serene. Bodies wracked with emotions that make the blood gush wildly through the veins, which throb impatiently, blaze with desire, shudder expectantly, struggle to hold back fear. Or bodies that hint at nights spent in purification, calming labours, caresses that bring contentment and composure. Lissom bodies in clothes that still owe something to childhood. Bodies that hide nothing, and simply dissemble. Bodies that quiver in the wind, in anger, in delight. Bodies nourished by red-hot sap, blossoming with smiles and sin.

I caress them with my eyes, steal from each and every one of them. Made smaller by drooping eyelids, within the dark rings of insomnia, shedding hypocritical, myopic tears and hidden by disgusting, deforming lenses, my eyes are never noticed. No one suspects how much lust, how much cruelty, how much hate they conceal. No one has ever noticed these glances of mine, which steal flesh, expose bodies, bite virgins. I'm ugly, my lips are pale and pinched, my bones are brittle. The bodies I see avert their gaze from my disfigured face. These bodies are looking for rosy cheeks and thick, red, fiery lips, big blue eyes or big dark eyes, and arms that know how to caress. What do I have to offer the enchanting bodies that appear to me on street corners awash with sunlight?

More and more I hide myself in ash-grey clothes; I'd like to be a speck of dust, to always go unnoticed. Because the contempt from these bodies fills my soul with pain.

But it won't be long before things change. I'll speak. I'll draw close to these bodies in their enticing garments and I'll speak, and they'll feel the heat of my words, the red-hot embers of my being will sear their flesh. And then they'll call out to me, and love me. I might not have beautiful eyes or cherry lips to offer them, but my body will be like a rock, my virile limbs will grind and pound, my muscles will tense and pulse like a knot of strangled snakes.

I'll give off a cloud of sparks that melts any last, remaining doubts. My gestures will bear witness to my insatiable desires, my caresses will be refined and brutal, like a sex that delights and dominates.

I will speak. And what body will resist me? What hands will hold clothes to their breasts when my fingers sink into them to conquer their flesh? What thighs will refuse to open? What eyes will dare meet mine? My lips will bite, my arms will pummel the convulsing body while my steely chest crushes white breasts. My body will be spattered with blood. And my victory will leave my partners exhausted at my side, their eyes filled with astonishment.

My pleasure will be the pleasure of an aroused, impassioned male. No beautiful face, no colourful clothes. Simply sex, a lively rhythm, a steadfast gaze, a foamy outpouring of desire. A virility free of the shackles of libido. A virility that shines like the stars above.

As I steal scowling through the streets, these thoughts console me. My fury subsides. My visions make me smile. The vision of my victory over all the rest...

I'm plotting my revenge against the bodies that treat me with disdain and disgust, them and their perverse, devilish refinements. In years to come they'll seek me out. Already I'm undressing them, weighing their charms, dominating them. And deep down I smile.

Then I'm back in the street, all alone. And I walk on, my determination growing, my eyes fixed on the ground. No one must notice me, no one must suspect me. I walk in the shade of the chestnut trees. With me go my visions. I conceal them within me, to urge me on. Occasionally I imagine that I have reached the mountain top, and in my mind I stop to rest. And a feeling of blessed languor gradually penetrates my flesh.

But soon I wake up. I'm not there yet. I'm still climbing through the thorn bushes, my mind clouded with visions. My hollow cheeks fill with gloom. Shaded from the light, my eyes sparkle. Secretly, unseen, my fists clench. I feel the blood pulsing in my neck.

And I decide not to wait till Saturday.

Papini, Me and the World

Today I read *The Failure* by Giovanni Papini. I'm a failure too. My novel will never make it onto the page. And I also have to change. I have to, or people will accuse me of being like Giovanni Papini.

I've had a love-hate relationship with him all afternoon. I hate him because he's already said things that I'd like to say myself. And I love him because his book describes my life. A childhood poisoned by suppressed rage, by jealousy for people with pretty faces, hatred of the rich and powerful, as well as those who are happy. An adolescence tortured by myopia and mental obsessions, eaten up by wild ambition, scourged by impotence, consumed by tears that no one heard or suspected, and never helped me to dry.

I've lived the life of Papini. I've also wept, I've whipped myself, I've cried out in my solitude, and I've been filled with untrammelled joy when I read *The Failure*. I was that man. But I wasn't a failure. I couldn't be. If Papini used up all the treasures that lay glittering in the depths of his soul – treasures that also glitter in my soul – it holds no terrors for me. I'll create a new soul and set off in search of new roads to travel. I don't want to be another Giovanni Papini.

Today, just before sunset, *I died*. From now on, a different light will shine on my disfigured face. My clouded eyes will see the world in a different way, and another life will rise up from the depths of my soul.

I don't want to be Giovanni Papini. I don't want to be someone else. I don't want my shoulders to bear the burdens of others. I don't want to suffer other people's pain. And I don't want to follow in someone else's footsteps.

Papini is ugly, terribly ugly, and he's short-sighted. I'll be handsome, I'll bewitch the ladies, I'll have a clear and penetrating gaze.

I'll slap my hollow cheeks until I feel the blood tingling painfully beneath my skin. I'll smash my glasses and widen my eyes until they're big, really really big. Clear eyes. Dark eyes, if Papini's are green. And green eyes if his are dark.

This will be my aim in life: to be different from Papini. Not to look like him; not to be him.

Papini is now my mortal enemy. He stole the treasures of my soul. He blackened, consumed, trampled, violated and prostituted the values that I was meant to proclaim to the world. He dissected and laid bare the putrefaction of his soul. And in doing so he raised himself up, became great, reached the summit, the place that *I* was supposed to reach. All I could have done, all I could have created, has been created by Papini. My God has poured the hot coals and the ice of a perverse joke over my head. I'm just a piece of rag in the hand of the Demiurge. I'm the mask of clay that was thrown into the world twenty years after the original was made. I was created to slither like a worm at the feet of my master: Papini. I was created to plead for my life, broken and ruined, at the feet of my master: Papini.

The masses and the morons, the imbeciles and the mentally ill, the simpletons with beautiful eyes and narrow brows, the creatures who compromise their sex, all those young men who deserve to get my fist, and the fists of a few chosen ones like me, in their faces, will never understand the tragic pain and suffering of my life. They'll accuse me of aping Papini. Of doing, of my own free will, those things that make me similar to Papini. That I'm nothing but an epigone, a shadow, a foolish Balkan reflection of the man from Florence.

But this won't happen. I don't give a damn about the craven will of the Creator. I don't give a damn about what becomes of me. I don't give a damn about myself.

Soon I'll be another person. I'll show people that the river of my soul can flow into different seas. Everywhere I go I'll bear new fruit. I'll shine a light into new places of darkness and, bleeding and torn, I'll climb new flights of stairs. What does it matter if I've damaged my eyes reading books, filling notebooks, creating indexes that won't be of any further use to me? What does it matter if I've wasted years preparing for things I'll never achieve? What do my aspirations, my joys, my sufferings and my vendettas matter? They've all faded away, along with the setting sun. They've faded, far far away from my soul. They've fallen into dark waters, and I look down on them and smile.

My real life is only just beginning. And so is my real struggle. The struggle against Papini, the World, and the Demiurge. And the struggle against myself: the fiercest of all.

Papini has been my most ruthless enemy and my most generous friend. While reading him I was both tormented and filled with delight. I found myself. Quite unexpectedly, a light shone into the depths of my soul. Life demanded different prices from me. Prices that I had already glimpsed, but hadn't dared face up to. Papini helped me to be myself. Papini taught me to stride boldly into the light and cry: 'Look! This is me.' From now on I won't be afraid of other people. Any doubt that was seeping from my soul has vanished. I shall hold my head up and spit my laughter and my venom into the face of the crowd.

What, up till now, has been trembling fearfully inside me, has begun to thunder with a deafening roar. I have suddenly been overwhelmed by forces beyond my control. I feel life pulsing through me so wildly that the sight of those around me fills me with terror. They all seem so powerless, insignificant and drab. In the faces of people who pass me in the street I see only a risible reflection of myself in miniature.

ME! Only now do I understand its true worth, all the gold, all the divine gifts that are secretly contained within that terrifying and seductive word.

ME! Only now do I understand my desires, my ceaseless efforts, my pain. Papini gave me rose-tinted glasses with which to see the world, and thrust me onto this hard and narrow road. But I'm not afraid. My muscles are strong and my bones are solid, my blood flows hot, mightily and red, and the stale slops of adolescence will no longer seep into my soul. No longer will an autumn twilight or foolish visions fill me with dread. My body will be constantly poised, ready to launch itself higher and higher. And in my soul I will preserve the same masculine tumescence, and the seed of my thoughts will fertilize furrows without number. Because I have such riches in abundance; I have no need to fear that one day I will dry up, and will have to beg from other people. In the depths of my soul there flows an endless, foaming torrent, just awaiting the order to pour out into the world. The day of the blood-red dawn is nigh. And then who will dare challenge me? Who will dare approach me, without fear of my smouldering eyes and thoughts? What snail will detach itself from the mob and attempt to drag its slimy being towards my haunches? I'd like to see my friends and my enemies, to look into the eyes of the thousands of human wrecks who roam the streets. I'd like to see them tremble as they bow down to the ground in submission. How they'll writhe in agony, their entrails seared by the burning poison of envy and crippled impotence.

I fear no one. I'm ready to show anyone my gold and my jewels. Even Giovanni Papini. And I'd like to hear someone dare accuse me of plagiarism, that my novel is an imitation of *The Failure*. I'd like to meet the man who doubts the power of my flesh and my mind. He'll find that I'm a short-sighted adolescent buried beneath a mountain of books in my attic. So let him come, with his jealousy and peevish questions. I'll make him welcome, let him run his paws over my innermost thoughts, turn out the drawers of my desk, prod my old wounds. And perhaps, eventually, as night begins to fall, one of us will smile.

A Year

A year has passed.

A year has passed, and I haven't written a word in my notebook. Why should I write? *The Diary of the Short-Sighted Adolescent* seems a waste of time. Every time Dinu reminds me about it and my other plans, I laugh. The glory of being a young, up-and-coming novelist holds no attraction for me anymore.

A year has passed. And not one of us has died, although it feels as if many of us are dead. I've re-read everything I've written so far. How distant some things seem now, while others are so strange... I've lived with all of them, almost every day. Yet if I look back over my life as it was two years ago, and over the past year, I realize how much we and our souls have changed.

My friendship with Robert has cooled. It happened gradually, almost without us realizing. He thinks I'm pedantic, I think he's naïve. He bores me, while I annoy him. He visits me less and less often. And when he does come to see me we have nothing to talk about. But because he doesn't know what else to say, he always asks me the same question: 'What are you reading?'

And I point to the book in front of me. And we look at each other distrustfully. He tells our friends that I'm a victim of my own erudition. I speak ill of him all the time.

Nor are we classmates any longer. Along with Furtuneanu and Bricterian he went to a private school for his final year, and they all failed their exams. The other two retook them and passed, and are now at university. But Robert didn't want to spend another year at a lycée. So instead he went to the Conservatoire, like Bricterian, and wears bizarre clothes in order to draw attention to himself.

A year. Sitting staring at this notebook, I feel so confused. What can I write? What has been *most important* to me this year? It passed just like that, one event after another, they affected me then I forgot about them. I continued to read and write. And I became more and more isolated. The others stopped off at places that I'd prefer not to contemplate. They let me move on, all alone. Some of them regard me with suspicion. Meanwhile I've turned in on myself more and more. And I haven't found a soulmate, not a single one.

But this shouldn't grieve me in any way. I'm going to become increasingly isolated. Isn't it better that way? Isn't that what I really wanted?

Yet I can look back on the spring that has just gone by without causing myself any pain. A spring that I spent almost completely in the library. Warm afternoons and tranquil evenings, blood-red sunsets that filled the room with their melancholy light. And I was there on my own or with Marcu, and we would see young couples, and students, and my thoughts would turn to the university, to the Greek I would have to learn, which would tire my eyes and take up the best years of my life.

There were so many thoughts, and I felt things so deeply in my soul, but I didn't have anyone to confide in. Perhaps I suffered a great deal, but I told myself that that this wasn't suffering, that this was happiness: solitude.

That's how spring went by, sitting staring at the same enormous, green, leather-bound book that no one requested any more. Then summer came, the afternoons got even hotter and longer, the female students wore flimsy white dresses, they were pretty and always smiling, while I was ugly and read the same book without ever raising my eyes. Why should I? And beside me sat Marcu. We smiled when beautiful girls walked past, and on the way home we discussed them.

And now another springtime is drawing to a close, and still I sit in the library waiting for evening to come, and then walk home alone. I keep telling myself that I'm happy. But don't I know that this isn't happiness?

I've changed a lot. I've realized that I have to lead a double life. That's why I'm not the same when I'm with my friends as when I'm alone. I've tried many times to discover who I am. But I didn't succeed, and that made me very sad. Yet the next morning I was completely self-aware. This was a great comfort to me.

Dinu is more handsome than ever.

Perhaps I'm only writing this because I feel I should write as much as I can in my *Diary*, to make up for a whole year. But how do I know what happened over the course of a year? I spent every morning looking forward to going to the library. Once in the library I was no longer myself. I was someone who read. While reading, I would become unconscious of my surroundings. That's why all those hours spent in the library seem so strange, I can't place them in the flow of time. It's extremely difficult to identify here the subtle differences that I discovered about the 'me' in the library and the 'me' during the rest of the day. It's only in the latter that it becomes possible to perceive time. That is where memories are found, nowhere else. But it's so barren. So much time spent reading that now I have hardly a single memory of the entire year. I don't know what happened to the winter, I don't know how spring came. All that remain are one or two days of the Easter holidays, and a few weeks during the summer. Apart from that, nothing.

Every night I would fall asleep thinking of the book I had left on the table. Every morning I woke up regretting that I had wasted so much time while the book was still unfinished. My thoughts were only on the future, I wished only for more books, and everything I did, I did for the future. And the days went by one after another, dull, grey, monotonous, lit only by the this same desire.

When did I see the first flower? And when did I smile as I watched a white butterfly? When did I feel sad, overwhelmed by those cold, red sunsets that trickled down the walls and turned the boulevards the colour of blood?

Petrişor is at university now. We see each other occasionally, and he tells me all about it. I greatly enjoy listening to him, and think about how it won't be long before I'm a student too, leading the life of a student.

But I know that that's not how it will be.

During this year, nearly all my friends have fallen in love. Not one of them has escaped. Except me. I'm delighted about this, and tell myself it's a sign of virility. But don't I know that when I say this I'm lying to myself, and bite my lip to stop myself crying? And don't I know that when I force myself to smile and mock those who are in love that I'd also like to be in love, because my heart is overflowing with a whirling, boiling mass of love?

But today I feel sad. That's why I've written so many useless pages. I closed my book so I could read my 'novel', and now I'm wasting time with it, suffering like an adolescent. The truth is that today I'm sad, which is to say an idiot. But tomorrow I'll be strong as always, and I'll put up a fight. And after the fight will come the victory. All this lamenting over a year that is past, a year during which I read two hundred books, is worthy of a hero from a novel by Ionel Teodoreanu.

It's true that I get tired occasionally. That's when I feel faint, and write these sentimental, sucrose, doleful pages. But they're completely false. If I were to re-read them when I wake up at dawn, I'd laugh. Such sad moments are fleeting. I either set them aside deliberately, or the life that is within me does it for me. I can feel it, this life, boiling in my veins, my chest, my temples. A life that not one of my friends ever experiences. A life that grows and becomes stormy, that foams and bubbles, that boils, that grows, that threatens, that shakes the foundations of my being. A life that I find very difficult to conceal, but which I experience whenever I'm alone, and which fills me with the thrill of battle and victory. Those who tell me that I'll be a man of learning are mistaken. All they see in my erudition is erudition. But I understand. I know that beneath all this lies something else: raw desire. And I shudder at this desire of mine, shudder at the thought of it being unleashed on the world.

That's why the sad moments are fleeting. They're just shadows in my powerful, passionate life that surges up from deep inside me. No one suspects what my life is really like. But I won't be able to hide it for much longer.

A year has passed and I am left with very few memories. It's better that way. What would I do with memories? Memories are a sign of wasted time. I didn't waste my time. I worked. Continuously, persistently, patiently, fired by a sacred thirst for knowledge, penetrated by the tremblings of my inner life. Work that I accomplished with a groan, a gasp, a cry of victory or pain, gnashing or gritting my teeth, my face contorted or expressionless, my eyes fixed constantly on my goal. At night I fell asleep regretting all the hours I would have to spend motionless in bed, sighing or snoring. Or I dozed off from exhaustion, my eyelids drooping, my brow hot and clammy. And I woke in the cool of the dawn, curled up in my nice warm bed, but my body rebelled and got up. Shivering, I put on some clothes and sat at my desk. My face dried, my eyes took on a bluish tinge and sunk into their sockets, and the furrows on my brow grew deeper.

These are the little victories that I've won day after day, and which have vanished from my mind. But I have to remember them. Otherwise, my year will have been barren and empty. And people will accuse me of leading a boring life and label me a bookworm. But they know nothing of my passions, my doubts, my fears, my struggles or my victories. Yet this was my year. For me there was no love, no friendship, no bucolic twilights, no melancholic autumn, no mournful calling of cranes, no dreamy contemplation of the sea, no pleasures of the flesh. Or – if I did experience them – I've forgotten them. Because I wanted to. I wanted to forget them. In which case my year is a wasteland of futile, sentimental frippery, an empty, monotonous and feeble waste of time. But it was still my year, the year of my desires, which I've infused with my blood, quickened with my life, tempered with my thoughts. The fruit it has borne are mine and mine alone. And tonight, as this miracle is revealed, I am proud of my miracle. I glorify myself, sing my own praises. Because I alone am the master of my body, I am the God of my soul. The One omnipotent master, God.

IV

Friends

I've been so isolated for the past few months that I began to think that I had almost no friends at all. I realize that our different aims have forced us apart, that we have forged links with other lives. This might have upset me were it not for the fact that I wanted to be alone. My path has led me away from my friends, while their paths have led them away from me.

And yet here we all were today, together again in my attic, everyone from the good old days of our adolescence. We talked about things that had only just happened, and how they seem such ancient history now, so old and sad.

But we didn't allow ourselves to be overcome by our memories, we all felt the need to talk about them, to admit that we are bound together by the same sense of melancholy.

We were here to celebrate a visit from Radu. He has run away from boarding school in Brașov, because he knew he was going to have to repeat a year. It's the second time this has happened. Up till now we've always met during the holidays, him in his drum-shaped cap, short-sighted, with huge teeth and big, cracked lips. He has learnt some Hungarian expressions and German jokes. To make him feel better we all laughed. But our friend is like a fish out of water.

He drinks țuica in the morning, smokes fifty cigarettes a day, and tells silly stories. With every holiday he gets more and more foolish. Up there in Brașov, where he sneaks out of the dormitory after midnight and comes back straight from the pot-house, drunk and bleeding, he has lost his good character, his sparkling wit, his talent for observation and caustic remarks. He has made friends with a landowner's son who is as stupid as he is strong, and who is the terror of all the local nightspots and forces his friends to drink alcohol by the bottle under threat of physical violence. He has become cynical and vulgar. He can't eat or sleep without ţuica.

And now he has run away. He told us quite calmly about the welcome he got from his father, who made a scene, and first threatened then pleaded with him. Radu remained unswerving: he didn't want to go to any more schools. He said he would only start studying again when his heart was in it. But for now, *he simply couldn't study*.

'Because Mama has just died...'

Immediately the attic was filled with a profound silence.

Radu smoked a cigarette, and looked slightly embarrassed. And then I saw the resigned and bitter expressions on the others' faces, filled with more pain than a night of tears. No one had been expecting this remark. We had only seen our friend on the day of the funeral, just after he got off the train. He had looked bored and tired. Not once had he shed a tear, or sighed. He was smoking.

'I knew she would die...'

We were appalled.

'What a cynic.'

Then all of a sudden, from among our murmuring there appeared a new face and a new soul. I would have liked to cry, to cry with him, to comfort him. My friends seemed very upset. Then his joke promptly broke the strange, awkward silence. Without looking at him, we all smiled. And it occurred to me how pointless it is, this *Diary* where I sketch out characters that I stumble across, without any form of continuity, badly, inaccurately, in fact deliberately so. It saddened me to see how little we knew about each other, for each of us has secrets that we never reveal. It sometimes happens that a sunset, a walk in the moonlight or a moment of great joy in springtime will suddenly shine a light into the darkest recesses of the soul, for those who are able to see it. At these times I clasp my friend's arm and keep my secret to myself. And I smile whenever I realize how strange my friend must appear to others, how they might think his behaviour is like that of a madman.

After we had listened to Radu's jokes, one by one we began to talk about our plans for the future. There was only a month to go till the exams. The new Baccalaureate filled us with dread: we would be the first year to take it. Those who in the past have simply swotted are now pushing themselves to the limit. No one knows exactly what the Baccalaureate consists of. The masters are all nervous, while the boys are absolutely terrified. Instead of a kind, friendly committee chosen from among the teachers at our lycée, who have known us since we were young children, we will go before a series of strict examining boards who will take three minutes to weigh us in the balance, and decide whether we are good enough for university or not.

Fănică is horrified at the thought of the big exam. He hasn't made any plans at all for the future.

'Only to hold a diploma in my hand...'

But we are still brave enough to laugh. We envy Furtuneanu and Bricterian, who are now students, one reading Law and the other Philosophy.

'After the Baccalaureate I'll have a party, and then it's Law School here I come!'

This is what Fănică says. He's afraid to assume that things will turn out well. What if he fails? We remind him that his tendency to become highly emotional could be fatal. Fănică bangs his fist against the corner of the table, a look of terror on his face.

'Stop playing the prophet of doom, it'll bring bad luck!'

Robert wants to be an actor at the National Theatre and a university lecturer in French Literature. We don't waste the opportunity to make fun of him.

'Just as long as you don't muddle up the two roles, and give a lecture at the university as if you're playing the juvenile lead.'

Robert gives a superior smile. He says that his teachers at the Conservatoire predict a bright future for him.

'And as for university, you all know my abilities...'

'Oh yes, we know! We know!' we all hurriedly reply in unison.

'I won't have any difficulty getting a chair in French language and literature...'

We remember how Robert first started reading French, with two books that Dinu had given him; how he had borrowed my Balzac, how he became enamoured with Faguet's criticism, how he learnt Musset off by heart, how he 'understood' Corneille after reading a monograph about him. Each of us had half-forgotten details to dust off. Like Robert in short trousers in a class photograph taken when we were in the Fourth Form. Our minds went back to when we were small, discovering books, lending them to each other, writing in our first *Diaries*, struggling to get our first, anonymous pieces published in literary reviews. The others remembered my passion for science, which was long spent. Each of us had his clutch of memories left over from a childhood and adolescence spent in a lycée and an attic.

We talked away so happily. So why am I feeling so despondent now, so overwhelmed by sadness and despair?

The others asked me how I was getting on with my novel. I lied, and told them that I was on the second part. But surely I know that I'll never finish *The Novel of the Short-Sighted Adolescent*, because my memories and observations will never make a novel? They asked me to read a few chapters. I gave them some fragments from this notebook. I told them that this impromptu gathering of ours – perhaps the last time we would get together before leaving school – would be the subject of a whole chapter.

And then, when I began to speak, they all stopped interrupting and making comments. I don't know why, but I was feeling very emotional. Forcing a smile, I told them that we would now go our separate ways, and that our friendship of the last eight years would simply come to a close. We would make new friends, some of them might be girls. And, who knows, maybe today would mark the end of a stage in all our lives.

So a Baccalaureate party, like we'd been planning for years, just wouldn't happen. A lot of us wouldn't pass the Baccalaureate in the summer, and would have to retake it in the autumn. And even then, how many would get through the second attempt? But we would meet up again in five years time.

'I think we'll be far unhappier than we might imagine...'

As I spoke these last, gentle words, my eyes ran along the shelves full of books. Why was I suddenly seized with premonitions of death?

I didn't even have the presence of mind to reproach myself for this melancholic outburst. Bricterian, Radu and Furtuneanu sat sadly on the edge of the bed.

Nostalgically they looked round my little room.

'How long have we been coming to this attic?'

'Eight years.'

Radu lit a cigarette, his eyes filling with tears. But he was obviously thinking about his dead mother. The others leafed through magazines. Marcu laughed, an affront to our sad thoughts. But I understood, and gave him a discreet little smile. Only Fănică was unaffected.

'See, they're crying! They're all crying!'

This annoyed us, so we decided to change the subject. By now it was getting dark. Through the open windows came the squealing of the trams out on the boulevards.

None of us had the courage to leave. The thought of not seeing each other again left us confused and disconcerted.

By the middle of May, however, we were drawn into the streets, to stroll under the chestnut trees in the cool of evening. And then on to the Cişmigiu Gardens and the main avenue, like we had in previous summers, before my friends and I went our different ways.

I put out the lamp and we went down the wooden stairs without saying a word. We spent a while in the garden, with all its flowers. It was a long time since the eight of us had been together in my attic.Then we said goodnight, and everyone made their way home.

So now I'm sitting here, all alone again. It's the first time I've started to be frightened by the thought that this attic won't always be mine. I look at it, study it, let my gaze rest on its every corner.

I certainly know that summer is here. I'm feeling so sad and tired, so depressed. Of course, it's just a bout of melancholy. I'll be happy when my schooldays are finally over.

But this isn't the time to be thinking about all that. I should be glad that I've found a new friend in Radu. Perhaps he won't get bored talking to me, long into the night.

But I shouldn't be thinking about that, either. I should be concentrating on the Baccalaureate. I'm sure that Vanciu will fail me...

Who knows when I'll write in this notebook again?

Summer Sorrows

Here I am, alone again. Everyone left school, happy to have passed the Baccalaureate or hoping to do so in the autumn. I failed – as usual, – so now I'm waiting till I've got some money or pluck up the courage to leave. It's hot, and I spend my time in other parts of the house, which remind me of my childhood and the games I used to play, and of my brothers, who now live far away.

I find it almost impossible to read. But I'm not sad, and I'm not filled with bitter thoughts about the pitiful end to my school career. If I think back seriously, there were so many wasted years when my face was just as gaunt, and my glasses just as uncomfortable. But I passed through the final frontiers of adolescence a long time ago. So I know that whining and self-indulgent melancholy are utterly pointless.

But the truth, the simple, unvarnished, unsentimental truth, is that I'm tired. I'm bored and oppressed by this finale that seems to be perversely prolonging its own death-throes. I'd like to know – whatever the risk – this very second, precisely what fate has in store for me. I'll either go to university this year, or I'll waste month after disillusioned month, waiting to take another exam.

Not only that, I'm exhausted by the secret struggle that I wage without hope of a swift victory. When will it be over? Will there still be glints of it in my eye on the day of judgement? And who will judge me?

I have a feeling that this summer – spent tragically suffocating in rooms beneath a blazing hot roof – will be the last. How bizarre that sounds... for I'm not thinking about death. I know that I have to live for a long time, because I'm filled with so much hatred. But I think my spiritual tribulations are coming to an end, and that I will soon acquire a different viewpoint, which will allow me to see the world in new ways.

From now on I won't be inventing 'memories' for myself. I'll stop wearing my black tunic and won't be tormented by all those silly little temptations. I've deserted my friends, and they've deserted me. Whenever we meet, we laugh, we flatter each other and wonder about the future, the same as always. But I'm well aware that we only do this because it's all we can do. And that whatever our inner lives once had in common no longer exists.

This tears my soul asunder, just like it does to my friends. I can feel them going, one by one, and my soul becomes more and more barren, more devoid of love for my fellow human beings.

There are so many faces that I'll never see again, so many habits that I'll lose, only to acquire new ones.

And even this adolescence that I've lived through, wallowed in, and rebelled against, will now be consigned to the past so I can insinuate my way into côteries of conceited young men with long hair. I'm tempted to feel sad about it. So many years, so much pain, so many hopes.

I don't know what lies in store for me *on the other side...* Will I make new friends? Will I have to change again, change so profoundly that I'll look into the mirror and not recognize myself?

I know nothing at all, and my heart is filled with fear. I'm afraid I'll have to stop being myself. I'm afraid of myself, of life. And yet I go on suffering as I wait to find out, wait to discard the ragged clothes of this world, clothes that I have long outgrown, and to which I am still attached by the most squalid of chains.

It's hotter than ever now, and I'm still just as alone. I only go out at night and avoid other people, wander the boulevards and the Cişmigiu Gardens, telling myself: 'How beautiful life is!' And then I wonder, disconsolately, if I have a reason to live. And I don't know.

What am I missing? What am I missing?

I re-read my notebooks with all my memories. All that seems so far away now... my friends, my 'characters', have changed so much. As for me, I'm a stranger. I pretended to be happy, and even hid from myself. But how can I be sure that what I'm writing now is actually the truth?

Summer .. I'm left alone to finish the struggle, while the great host of my enemies rises up from within me. I don't know what

I'm fighting against, but I feel the pain of combat and the red-hot brand that cleaves me in two. Why did I want to be alone? Why is there no one by my side? No one, no one... on hearing these words, the soul falls silent.

Once again I think about these eighteen years that I've wasted. My legs carry me blindly into the night, where my eyes see only ghosts. The hours go by, and still I don't know if I've answered all the questions that my soul is asking. And then I come home again, where I wander from room to room, my mind sinks deeper and deeper, and the years are scattered before me and I stare at them.

I can't do any school work. And I wonder how I'll ever get in to university. I wish it would rain, keep on raining day after day. I want for so little now.

The day of judgement will be truly painful. But I have to overcome this predicament as well. One morning, this silent, exhausting, tyrannical despair will disappear; and then I'll forget these summer nights with their scorching heat and sadness. I'll find I'm a different person with a clean, fresh soul, and my eyes will embrace the sun, fill themselves with it like a pitcher. And I'll settle my account with adolescence. My soul will be filled with so much bitterness, so many wounds will be reopened... I'll remember the nights that began for me in the Cişmigiu Gardens, envying other people their happiness and looking down at my sad, empty footsteps as I wandered the pathways. And all those longings that I succumb to even now, almost without putting up a fight. And the pain I've suffered at twilight, because I've felt so alone. And all these lines in my notebook, which is nearly full. Who will be the victor?

My adolescent jottings are coming to an end. When will I dare start my novel? Notebook after notebook has been finished, each one dated with a different month or year. Where are all these shadows now? Where are my desires, my fears, where are all my tears?

I have the feeling that everything I've believed in so far has gone up in smoke; that everything I've done is crumbling to dust; that my whole life has been a dream. Never before have I felt so estranged from myself.

I'm tired and depressed, all alone in this house weighed down with memories. Why am I so overwhelmed by memories? Why does the summer night surround me with the plaintive cry of crickets and the waning of passions? Has my strength abandoned me? Has my soul truly collapsed? Does it have to change? Do I have to change? Do I have to go out into the street, bend down and pick up help and love wherever I find them? Do I have to earn friends?

Everything that I have now come to understand fills me with pain to the deepest depths of my being. Am I so feeble that a single summer night can reduce me to such a state of collapse?

I'd love to know what I'll be feeling and thinking when next summer comes... And if my soul will finally allow me to cry.

VI

Buffeted by the Wind

But is *this* really all there is to the world?

For the past few days I've been tormented by questions of a *different* kind. How can I explain? It's as if something has been missing from my life for years, something profound, vast, definite and essential – something I could meld with. I could have had a friend by now. But I'm alone, seared by doubts that tear my soul asunder and dissipate my desires.

The days when I found solace in chemistry and insects are long gone. I don't think about them anymore, they're of no interest to me. Gone, too, are the days of Felix Le Dantec and Haeckel, which would end with me sitting innocently staring at my fish bowl full of newts, as are all those nights spent poring over the *Bibliotheque de Philosophie Scientifique*, with its red binding. Almost without me noticing, the foundations of my soul have been shifting. Things that I once valued, I now view with indifference. All those weeks during the autumn and winter that I thought were dull and pointless, and which I spent resignedly reading things that seemed irrelevant, have sown new 'seeds' in me. How can I describe them, if not as 'seeds?' I awoke enriched, brimming over, yet still tormented by the feeling that there was something missing, something I knew nothing about. Oh! It's so hard to write about things that I haven't learnt from books; I can't find the words, I don't know where to start...

But the end result of all those weeks is plain to see. I feel different; decidedly different. And yet it still distresses me that my sense of achievement, renewal and having surpassed myself is accompanied by one of absence, emptiness. I understand so little about the rays of light and dark that streak my soul. All I know is that during these years of crisis, they've become more intense.

I know they don't affect those adolescents who glide to *the other side* without encountering a single obstacle or moment of despair. And I assume that all this confusion will soon disappear, that the mist that hangs over my soul will lift; only then will I understand why all these changes were necessary.

That's why *The Novel of the Short-Sighted Adolescent* will never be written. How could I describe in words the bizarre movements of my soul? And even if I were to succeed, would my notebooks actually constitute a 'novel'? Could the five hundred pages that I've written provide enough material for even a few chapters? I've been gradually taking less and less notes about other people. I've tried to understand myself in depth, but haven't succeeded. Every time I look through my *Diary*, I'm horrified. I'm still a long, long way from a novel.

But as I write these words, I ask myself: would someone else be capable of producing a novel like mine, one that is a complete and accurate reflection of my adolescence, of our adolescence? More than anything I wanted to write a book that would give a full account of the inner life that I've lived on the fringe of school, of adolescence, an adolescence that I believed I was about to leave behind. I'll never succeed.

But who is this confession addressed to, all these things that I've known for so long? I've decided to stop writing in my *Diary*, because – without my 'novel' – there's no point. Every now and then, although increasingly rarely, when I'm feeling particularly sad or in the depths of despair, I open it, read a few pages, and occasionally add to it. I no longer collect material for it, and don't regard myself as a budding novelist, like I did last year. If someone were to read it, they wouldn't understand it. I haven't attempted to trace – and in any case, it would only be possible to do that in my imagination – the constantly changing forms of my soul. Any reader would see the hero as an endless contradiction.

I wonder how I got to this point: my major question, a novel about adolescence. It's a problem that can only be solved by giving up completely. Since I'm unable to even recognize myself on many pages of the notebook, and occasionally appear ridiculous and conceited, I asked myself how I managed to create a character for my novel who is so embarrassing and contradictory. I also wondered that if I were to make some alterations to the character in my *Diary*, I would still be realistic. And if my decision to not imitate reality is literary or not. I told myself: does the adolescent in the novel have to be a pupil at the Lycée Spiru Haret in 1924? Of course not. Nonetheless, I still wanted my novel to be based on real life, a personal confession, a settling of accounts.

I couldn't explain why I decided to write this kind of book about adolescence. Yet I can understand why I decided not to write any more when I realized how ridiculous the hero was. I was afraid that readers wouldn't see why I needed to ridicule adolescence, while still insisting on the need for heroism, nostalgia and mediocrity.

*

But I began by noting my spiritual state, which is as new as it is intense: one of utter discontent. This is no passing mood, like when books lose their flavour, but sadness hovering on the brink of despair. I don't recognize my soul as it is now from any of the sad 'chapters' in my *Diary*. I'm calm and relaxed. Yet I sense the inadequacy of my inner life, and feel constrained by horizons that I used to regard as wide and expansive. That's all it is; and yet it's a lot. I could go on saying it forever: is that all it is? Is that all it is?

I don't know why I'm so annoyed about my scientific work. I'm sure it was always done in a spirit of spontaneity, unhampered by rules; that's why I can't complain about the lack of any major results. Besides, I know so little now about fundamental things. Every time I want to find out the real *causes*, I feel so overwhelmed, dissatisfied, completely at sea. I'm convinced that I'm going down a dead end. The very thought of it fills me with frustrated rage, because I don't understand where this conviction of mine comes from.

One evening, after a period of intense self-scrutiny, I told myself that I should set aside these scientific questions until I was at university, and to content myself with history for now. But like everything else we read that doesn't shake us to the core, history is just a form of opium. Books force us to waste our time intelligently.

Yet this intelligent waste of time is no less absurd than any other, because it leaves us exhausted and alienated from ourselves.

I now sense that science, history and philosophy are all pointless. I'm filled with a burning desire for a pure, single truth, the certainty of a faith, an infallible 'guide.' I don't know why, but I envy adolescents who are Roman Catholics.

And yet any Church is an anathema to me. Any dogma that I can't understand or explain infuriates me. After all the efforts made by science, it seems ridiculous to accept biblical nonsense and the horrors of Catholicism. But what if all these things *are not* the Church, in the same way I'm convinced they're not Religion?

I have an amateur interest in mysticism. I've read about the lives of Saints in the same way I've read other people's memoirs: out of curiosity. I've always been tirelessly curious, but if I were to become a monk, I'd still have a library of naturalist and erotic books. But I don't understand mysticism, although I came to the conclusion long ago that it doesn't have to be understood. I can't really share the spiritual life of the Saints, because I'm afraid of being converted by auto-suggestion, out of a desire to believe, and not from genuine evidence.

I'm not even sure if what I lack is faith. Every time I think of the word *faith*, I feel annoyed, even offended. I simply can't accept *faith* in God, in a Saviour, in Saints, or in a Church. In the past I was content with my open-minded attitude. But now it makes me uneasy; what if faith means *something else*? What if I haven't yet stumbled across the real significance of faith, and regard it as sinister superstition rather than something sublime that I'm too far away from to see?

But I'm straying from the path that I wanted to follow in this notebook. Nothing I've just said about faith is very clear or helpful... Perhaps I would express myself better if I pounded my fists against my forehead, closed my eyes and swore not to get up until I found an answer worth considering. But there's no point, at least for the moment. I'm anxious about this new vision that's come to me, I've no idea from whom or how long it's been happening, and almost no idea what caused it.

Today I was seized with a sudden and painful sense of dissatisfaction with myself and my work. When I asked myself: '*Is this life?* Is this all life is?' I actually meant: 'So *this* is all I've seen of life?' I no longer see anything in the books and aspirations that have filled me with enthusiasm in the past. It seems as if I lack an awareness of what the *point* of these books and aspirations really is. But why should I call them *mine*? Don't they stem from the fundamental needs of my soul? Aren't they actually my *authentic* soul, the soul I've always had?

Perhaps I've become estranged from my preoccupations. Perhaps I've had too many intensely personal experiences that have led me away from scientific books. But that's not a good enough explanation. I still have as much admiration for scientific books as before. Yet I ought to add something I wouldn't have said earlier: are these the kind of books that will fire my imagination, satisfy me and fill the rest of my life?

I've surpassed myself; that's for certain. I've come out of myself in order to move forward. With every book I've read, with every sorrow I've suppressed, I've taken a step in that direction. So why is the fact of surpassing myself so obvious today, and why, instead of being satisfied, am I saddened by it, overwhelmed by this feeling of absence? What am I missing? My inner life as I've experienced it so far, my visions, my aims, my values – why have they caved in all at once, without any reason, without a crisis of some kind?

Perhaps I've been building on sand, perhaps the material I've gathered is of no use. But are science, philosophy, and history of no use? I can't believe how far away they all seem now. So why the sudden collapse of the last few days, which has only just come to an end?

However hard I try, it won't make things any clearer. Despite all my theories and explanations, one fact remains: I am being buffeted by the wind.

I sense that I'm going to live through more than the simple experiences that you have while reading a book, or those undergone by a character in a book. I sense that I will offer up my entire inner life. But to whom? I can't imagine it will be the Church. I'm not a mystic, nor am I a fiendish, cynical, desperate atheist. So how can I come to Jesus?

This is what I feel: I've been taken out of myself and hurled against a lot of sharp corners, and then put back in my soul, and then taken out again. That's all I know, and I don't understand anything at all.

VII

The Baccalaureate

A slight attack of nerves during the retake. Marcu and I both give quick, detailed answers. After three years, Vanciu has managed to teach us maths. In the written exam we got all the questions right. We went home without any great excitement and now wait for the results.

Then came the anxious days that led up to the Baccalaureate. Many of those who retook it in the summer had failed, although only because of a few stupid questions. This didn't frighten me enough to make me spend the whole summer re-reading all the books from my last four years at school.

I tried to work out exactly what I needed to know, and what I knew already. I made a list of all the subjects, but the list never seemed never-ending, I didn't have much time, and my willpower began to waver. I told myself that the Baccalaureate was a test of general education, not the sort of details that anyone could memorize from books. I kept forgetting what my classmates – who had taken it in the summer – had told me about it. Marcu came over to my house so we could revise in the attic. I started with physics, while he did geography. But within an hour we were arguing about biology and literature. That's what always happens. So I revised physics by myself, and he did geography by himself. Then we met up again in the evening, and wandered off into passionate and cynical discussions, making plans for the work we would do at university, he in Medicine, me in Greek.

The results of the retake, registration for the Baccalaureate, which included a high fee, and the nerve-wracking wait for the exam itself, all these came and went.

Then it was autumn, and we were all seduced by the wistfulness of Bucharest, a tormented and melancholy city beneath a coverlet of dead leaves. We were humbled by the bright, cloudless mornings, by parks reinvigorated by the rain, by the narrow brown alleyways with their cold paving stones and white houses.

I slaved away at my revision, listening to the city outside the window, overflowing into the autumnal plains. Once again I didn't have the strength to laugh at myself for indulging in melancholia before such a major event. I would have liked to chase it all away somewhere, into the depths of my soul, into my native city, and to stride out heroically. And it occurred to me that I was a hero, for reading unbearable books during these first, gentle days of autumn.

In a room that was far too large and cold for us terror-stricken beings, we were allocated separate desks. Two masters we had never seen before hurriedly dictated the question to us. I calmed down as soon as I began to write. At the same time the following morning we had to translate a paragraph from the philosopher Seneca, and in the afternoon produce a French version. Then we had three days off. We went home full of joy, laughing in the streets, imagining we were already undergraduates. We treated Marcu to a chorus of anti-Semitic jokes. He replied sanctimoniously: 'The Jew lives forever!'

We all got through to the oral exam.

Sheets of white, official paper were posted on the noticeboard, giving the dates for all the exams. We were promptly overcome by a fever of frantic reading, nervous page-flicking, memorizing, writing revision cards and underlining with red pencils. I didn't recognize myself. I got up at dawn and pored over dry, daunting textbooks that I'd never opened in my whole time at the lycée. I worked with a mind and a spirit that were foreign to me, a determination that seemed to come instinctively. I could feel my strength fading, as if I was going to collapse and forget everything I had stored away.

And then all of a sudden I was calm, bored, filled with nausea. Devoid of emotion I waited for the oral exams.

...It's now evening, it's warm, and the air is filled with of the fragrance of rain. But this morning it was clear and cold. The leaves were falling, so were the ripe chestnuts, and the pavements were clean and violet-tinted. I left home without my cap or school bag. After Mama had kissed me, made the sign of the cross on my forehead, and lit a candle. I hadn't finished my cup of black coffee. I hadn't finished my croissant. Yet I wasn't nervous. I strolled along, avoiding the boulevards with their trams and hurrying people.

I was one of the first to arrive in the main courtyard. A few of my fellow candidates, from other lycées, were flicking through books that they took from bulging satchels. I didn't know anyone in my group. But Marcu and the others had promised to come and find out the result.

I wandered around, without thinking about anything, without wishing for anything. Every now and then I felt like shouting: 'Let's get on with it! Let's get on with it!...' But I calmed down and kept on pacing, without once looking at a book or revision card.

I remembered something that disconcerted me, a passing and seemingly mischievous remark made to me by a female medical student who was looking for my brother: 'I wish I were still at the lycée...'

And I remembered, and was disconcerted by, other half-forgotten scenes and words. I paced up and down the courtyard, my mind far away from the exam and the group of examiners who were taking their time to assemble.

After an hour we were summoned into a dark corridor. I looked round at my fellow candidates: they were trembling, white-lipped, with dry throats and lined brows. I had turned pale and was fiddling with my glasses.

The classroom was far too brightly lit. I was both surprised and annoyed to see there were no chairs. The examiners had chairs, while we sat side by side on a long bench. I felt calm; too calm.

We started with Romanian language and literature.

'What can you tell me about the evolution of suffixes?'

The boy stared blankly. His neighbour was trembling all over. I saw he was trying hard not to put up his hand. The first boy answered, but got confused. This delighted the third boy, who the examiner sadistically missed out, and moved on to me instead. I responded perhaps a little too quickly and sullenly.

'Can you give any examples from the Byzantine lexicon?'

It was a stupid question, but I knew the answer. Myopic and irritated, sometimes wearing a presumptuous smile, the examiner naturally assumed I was a prize-winning peacock, and asked me some other questions, whose answers couldn't be memorized. But he was hoist by his own petard, because I understood Eminescu, and interpreted the beginning of his 'Letter I' better than he had expected. He asked me about the Transylvanian historians, without suspecting that I had spent many a perfumed night reading Şincai, or knowing that I had recently found Şeineanu's *History of Romanian Philology* in a second-hand bookshop.

'Why did people persecute him so much?' This is what the others were probably wondering. Perhaps he was a Jew.

'What do you know about the origins of folk poetry?'

I told him what I knew. But he interrupted me.

'Thank you. I've heard enough from you.'

This first success encouraged me. When it came to history, I answered whatever questions the examiner's mistrustful curiosity required: such as Petru Muşat's[23] relationship with the Poles.

My neighbour wasn't quite so lucky.

'Where did Nicolae Mavrocordat enter Bucharest when he arrived from Moldova?'

'?'

'Which Romanian prince drowned in the Dâmboviţa?'

The last boy in the group knew the answer to this.

'Vlad the Drowned.'

'Do you know anything about him?'

'He was Voivode of Muntenia[24]...'

'Good.'

In geography I didn't know the name of a flower that grows on the north-eastern slopes of the Apuseni Mountains. Nor did I know the tributaries of the Crişul Alb. I got a four. The boys either side of me knew the names of so many rivers and mountains...

In physics and chemistry, as well as French, I was able to answer everything. It annoyed me that the examiner – an uneducated man – was only interested in synonyms and homonyms, or a summary of *El Cid*.

'Describe the evolution of the digestive system from echino-derms to man.'

I remembered my science lessons, the years spent in the physiology laboratories of the Casa Şcoalelor[25], my collections of insects, and my volumes of Brehm, Perrier and Fabre. The answer came to me slowly, gradually.

The question fascinated me; I made concerted efforts of memory, logic and concentration. But the examiner wasn't satisfied. He assumed that I just couldn't remember.

'If you start to learn something, you should finish it, like a proper know-all. As it is, I can only see evidence of average perseverance, for which you get a *five*.'

I went bright red. I was humiliated, furious, and upset. I would have liked to say: 'What?' I would have liked to challenge him – this supercilious, uneducated examiner whose knowledge had been acquired from elementary textbooks – to a debate about the philosophy of biology. But there was nothing I could do.

Bitterly, I swallowed my pride. But it was over.

I left the building without any feelings of delight, without running down the street shouting like I had promised myself. I told my friends how furious I was with the natural sciences examiner. They said I was naïve. And that *five* was a good mark.

I jotted down some figures on a wall and worked out the average. Come what may I'll get a six. I'm virtually certain to pass. But I don't feel the least bit glad, and that hurts; it hurts so much. Which is why I'm writing in my notebook: so I won't forget the pain I felt on the day of the exam.

In my novel, if I ever write it, I'll include all the foolishness, all the absurdity of the Baccalaureate. Using many examples I'll show that only the lucky ones pass, the favoured ones, the imbeciles. I've never seen the list of questions that everyone talks about. If they had asked me about *insects* in Natural Science, *Romanticism* in French, and *the geological origins of mountains* in Geography, I would have got the highest marks. If they had asked me anything else, I might have got an 'Unsatisfactory' in everything. So I'm lucky, but also unlucky. If I pass I'll just be average, by pure chance.

My shortcomings weren't discovered and my qualities weren't rewarded. How distressing...

And if I don't pass?...

It has just started to rain: heavy, cold, monotonous.

Is it autumn outside, or is it autumn in my attic?

VIII

Finale

I did it! I did it!

I'm the only one from our lycée to pass. It upsets me that Marcu didn't pass. We won't be friends anymore. What connected us was our minds, not our souls. Once we're apart, we might just forget about each other...

*

Anxiously, I found my name on the list. Then once again I walked through the large courtyard with its plane trees, as I had on the days of the exam. All of a sudden I was overcome by a powerful urge to see the lycée where I had spent eight years of my life. The masters and the pupils all asked me about the Baccalaureate. I gave brief answers. It made me sad to see classrooms where there would soon be no familiar faces. And it made me sad to see the school porter, and the little organ hidden under the stairs, and the shelves full of books that I'd read so many times...

My friends all kissed me...

It was now the time of gifts.

Who knows what life will bring during these days of autumn, when I feel so different, so strange, always on the point of crying, running, laughing?... I don't want to think about university. This is still an adolescent's notebook. I want to write a few more pages, and then finish it *once and for all.*

Who can really understand the devastating sadness I feel when I say *finish it once and for all*? a life is coming to an end. One day I'll look through this notebook, or perhaps I won't, and then – just like now – I'll be alone.

I find it hard to write. I get distracted by new pleasures, new ideas: university... and yet I'm still attached to my adolescence, to the novel I haven't written.

I haven't written it because I couldn't find a novel in myself or in other people. We were all just vague outlines, sentimental and mediocre. Sometimes ridiculous, sometimes heroic. How could I find a conflict in the world, one that would inspire a novel?

I haven't written it, and life weighs heavily on me, the life of the adolescent that would be described in my novel.

I don't understand anything that's going on around me at the moment. This novel obsesses me, I'm tormented by all the things that have to be said. Yet I don't know how to write it, I'm unable to write it.

*

The sun has come out again.

The sun has gone behind cloud.

Today I wandered through fields that smelt of autumn, just like I used to on childhood afternoons. I saw so many things that I haven't seen for a long time. And, standing next to a tree, I cried like an adolescent when I noticed a patch of blue sky. I didn't know why, and I didn't wonder why.

Then I came home.

From now on I'll have to work hard, without rest, never sparing myself or my youth. Yet I can't work. I hit myself, I bite my lip, but I just can't work...

*

Autumn, blood-red autumn, is coming to an end.

My attic is the same as ever: quiet, lonely, sad. I'm going to write *The Novel of the Short-Sighted Adolescent*. But I'll write it as if I'm writing the author's *Diary*. My book won't be a novel, but a collection of comments, notes, sketches for a novel. It's the only way of capturing reality, both natural and dramatic at once.

*

It's raining, it's still raining.

When you're in an attic, you always love the rain. I want to finish the *Diary* today, on this autumn day. I want to finish it because I'm burning to begin my *novel* now. I've already drafted the first few chapters.

I shall write: 'As I was all alone I decided to begin writing *The Novel of the Short-Sighted Adolescent* this very day...'

It's raining in the garden, and that makes me happy.

TRANSLATOR'S NOTES

1   *Fourth Form:* In the inter-war period, secondary education in Romania lasted for 8 years. It was, and still is, largely a lycée system, similar to that in France. The nearest UK equivalent to the year groups would be the more traditional terminology that is still used in many Independent Schools. Thus 'Fourth Form' is the year during which pupils reach the age of 14 (ie: Year 9 in the current British State system). This is followed by the Remove, the Fifth Form, the Lower Sixth and finally the Upper Sixth.

2   *Passion Week:* In the Orthodox Church, the week leading up to Easter. In the West it is usually referred to as Holy Week.

3   *Words and phrases marked with an asterisk* appear in French in the original text.

4   *ţuica:* a form of plum brandy very popular in Romania, and similar to slivovitz.

5   *oină:* a traditional Romanian sport, not dissimilar to baseball and the Russian game, lapta.

6   *bani:* the smallest unit of Romanian currency. There are 100 bani in 1 lev.

7   *doină:* an elegiac song typical of Romania, usually combining folk poetry and music.

8   *sârba:* a lively Romanian folk dance.

9   *Selma Lagerlöf... Blasco Ibáñez:* Selma Ottilia Lovisa Lagerlöf (1858-1940) was a Swedish author and the first female writer to win the Nobel Prize for Literature. She is best known for her children's book, Nils Holgerssons underbara resa genom Sverige (The Wonderful Adventures of Nils). Vicente Blasco Ibáñez (1867-1928) was a journalist, politician and best-selling Spanish novelist whose fame in the English-speaking world is for the Hollywood films adapted from his works.

10   *Marie Bashkirtseff:* Maria Konstantinovna Bashkirtseva (1858-1884) was a Russian diarist, painter and sculptor.

11   *Elzevir:* The House of Elzevir was a well-known family of Dutch booksellers, publishers and printers in the 17th and early 18th centuries.

12   *Înşir-te Mărgărite* and *Năpasta.* The first is a play by Victor Eftimiu, the second, as mentioned earlier, a play by Ion Luca Caragiale.

13   *abat-jour:* A lampshade. In French in the original text.

14 *tea-rooms:* In English in the original text.

15 *'Lalescu Scale':* In 1924, teachers in Romania demanded a 30% increase in academic salaries, significantly higher than those on the existing 'Lalescu Scale' of remuneration. Protests ensued.

16 *must:* new wine.

17 *Mosjoukine:* Ivan Illyich Mozzhukin (1889-1939) was a Russian film actor. His name usually appeared in publicity in the French transliteration, Mosjoukine, as used in Eliade's original text.

18 *Coteţ:* 'chicken coop' in Romanian.

19 *Fustel de Coulanges:* Numa Denis Fustel de Coulanges (1830-1889), French historian noted particularly for his work La Cité antique.

20 *Bună Dimineaţa la Moş-Ajun:* traditional song sung on Christmas Eve. 'Good Morning, Eve of Christmas'.

21 *'Sărut-mâna':* 'I kiss your hand'. A polite Romanian greeting from a man to a woman, still routinely used today, in much the same way as *'Küss die Hand'* in Austria.

22 *Facla:* an independent socialist newspaper founded in 1913 by Nicolae Dumitru Cocea, a journalist, novelist, critic and left-wing activist.

23 *Petru Muşat:* Petru I, Voivode of Moldova from 1367-1368.

24 *Muntenia:* a former Romanian feudal state, then a principality, and after that one of the united Romanian Principalities. It is now the Romanian province of Wallachia.

25 *Casa Şcoalelor:* the National School and Public Libraries Board.

THE AUTHOR

MIRCEA ELIADE was born in 1907 in Bucharest, the son of an army officer. He lived in India from 1928 till 1932, after which he obtained a doctorate in philosophy with a thesis on yoga, and taught at the University of Bucharest for seven years. During the war he was a cultural attaché in London and Lisbon, and from 1945 taught at the École des haut études in Paris and several other European universities. In 1957 he took up the chair of history of religion at the University of Chicago, a post that he held until his death in 1986. Fluent in eight languages, his extensive body of work includes studies of religion and the religious experience that remain influential, such as *The Sacred and the Profane*, and numerous works of literature, including *The Forbidden Forest*, *Bengal Nights* and *Youth without Youth*, both of which were adapted for the screen.

THE TRANSLATOR

CHRISTOPHER MONCRIEFF translates widely from French, German and Romanian literature. After military service in Europe, the Near East and the USA during the Cold War he produced large-scale son et lumière shows in Germany, France and Los Angeles before beginning to write and translate. He read Theology at Oxford and has qualifications in design and on the military staff. A frequent traveller in Central and Eastern Europe, he speaks a number of the languages of the region. He also works for autism organisations and is a neurodiversity activist.

istrosbooks

Istros Books is an independent publisher of contemporary literature from South E
Europe, based in London, UK. We aim to show-case the very best of literature from
region to a new audience of English speakers, through quality translations.

Our 2016 titles:

QUIET FLOWS THE UNA by *Faruk Šehić*

*An autobiographical novel by a veteran of the Bosnian war, this book is dedicated to pec
who believe in the power and beauty of life in the face of death and mass destruction. Wir
of the EU Prize for Literature and the Meša Selimović Award.*

BYRON AND THE BEAUTY by *Muharem Bazdulj*

*Loosely based on Byron's biography, this story takes place during two weeks of October 18
during his now famous sojourn in the Balkans. Besides being a great love story, this is c
a novel about East and West, about Europe and the Balkans, about travel and friends
and cruelty.*

LIFE BEGINS ON FRIDAY by *Ioana Pârvulescu*

*Set during 13 days at the end of 1897, this novel follows the fortunes of Dan Crețu, alias l
Kretzu, a present-day journalist hurled back in time by some mysterious process for just l
enough to allow us a wonderful glimpse into a remote, almost forgotten world. Winne
the EU Prize for Literature 2013.*

PANORAMA by *Dušan Šarotar*

*Follow the narrator's extraordinary travels around Europe as he tries to reveal the inner ex
rience of the writer in a foreign setting, far from a home that seems ever more elusive. In
manner of W. G. Sebald, this story is peppered with photographs taken by the author him*

THREE LOVES, ONE DEATH by *Evald Flisar*

*When one country is released from the oppression of a communist regime, one far
decides to make the best of the new-found freedom by starting a new life in the coutrys
But freedom also comes at a cost, a fact that Flisar beautifully illustrates in this sharp,
cinating story.*

NONE LIKE HER by *Jela Krečič*

*A light, scintillating, witty and positive novel exploring the pains of the thirty-someth
generation on their quest for identity. A debut novel from one of Slovenia's leading journal*

Supported using public funding by
**ARTS COUNCIL
ENGLAND**

LOTTERY FUNDED